Nettie's Secret Bodyguard

Cheryl Wright

Copyright

Nettie's Secret Bodyguard

Copyright ©2022 by Cheryl Wright

Small Town Romance Publications

ALL RIGHTS RESERVED

I will be forever grateful for all the singing and dancing lessons in my early life. Performing on stage over many years helped immensely in the writing of this book.

Dedication

To Margaret Tanner, my very dear friend and fellow author, for her enduring encouragement and friendship.

To Alan, my husband of over forty-eight years, who has been a relentless supporter of my writing and dreams for many years.

To You, my wonderful readers, who encourage me to continue writing these stories. It is such a joy knowing so many of you enjoy reading my stories as much as I love writing them for you.

Table of Contents

Chapter One

Late November, 1884 – Dalymore, Montana

Nettie Dupont sat in her dressing room preparing for tonight's performance.

There was no roar of the crowd, no applause hoping to entice her out, just the low mutterings of customers talking at their tables as they sipped their drinks. Together, Nettie and Ralph assessed this place almost the moment they stepped inside. They sensed it would not be conducive to their mental well-being, and Ralph decided he would play the piano until she made an appearance. Unfortunately, despite his excellent playing, no accolades were forthcoming.

No matter. They received the same fee, whether or not the audience listened.

It's what her head told her, but her heart said otherwise.

When she left home, Nettie had no idea she would end up here, a dive if ever there was one. But she was doing what she loved, and that was what mattered, right? Only she wasn't sure it was right. The daughter of an industrialist, her father discouraged her from taking up performing as a career. He told her it was not a career that would support her. Sadly, it seemed he could be right.

Not every place they'd played at was this bad. At most establishments they'd performed, they had an audience who listened, who cared, and even applauded them at the end of the show.

Right now, Nettie wanted to be anywhere but in this dump.

She sighed and continued to ready herself for the show. She pinned back her chestnut colored hair and added the clump of black feathers she'd fashioned into a headpiece. It helped her look the part. She was far from a burlesque dancer, but that's what her father had called her. He demanded she stop performing or leave home.

She chose to leave.

Her father wasn't a bad man. He loved her dearly, and Nettie loved him equally as much. He said if she left, her allowance would be cut off that very day.

Any sane person would say she was crazy, but Nettie was convinced she was being watched. Why anyone would spy on her, she didn't know, but it made her feel most uneasy.

The knock on the dressing room door distracted her. "Nettie, it's time." There was no stage manager in this place, and the barman doubled up for that job.

She pushed her chair back with a screech and headed to the backstage area. She peeked around the curtain, waited for Ralph to nod, then play a few bars to present her coming appearance, then Nettie stepped out onto the stage.

As she expected, there was no applause, no acknowledgement she was even there. She turned sad eyes to the audience and glanced across the darkened room. And there he was. He was slunk down in the corner, his hat pulled down over his face. It was glaringly obvious he was trying to hide his identity, and over the past weeks, he'd done exactly that.

She'd asked around, and no one could tell her who he was. No one knew. She watched as he lit a cigarette and took a sip of beer. With each movement, the man kept his face covered, and it made her wonder what he had to hide.

Nettie positioned herself ready to dance, holding the large feather fan across her face. She opened her mouth and sang, slowly dragging down the fan.

When she glanced his way again, the stranger was gone.

Ralph and Nettie sat at the café table sipping coffee. After a long night performing, they liked to unwind. There was a special buzz you got in front of an audience, and Nettie never tired of it.

"He was there again tonight," Nettie said between sips of coffee.

Ralph took a mouthful of carrot cake. "I saw him. He wasn't there long enough to see his face, though."

"Are you surprised? He never stays long." She flicked a stray clump of hair off her face. "I wish I knew what he wanted."

"Perhaps your father wants you to go back home."

Nettie couldn't help herself – she laughed out loud at his words. "He doesn't appreciate what we're doing." She glanced up and their mystery man strolled past, glancing at her for only a moment. She shoved her chair back and ran after him, but the stranger was gone before she was outside the café door.

Sighing as she sat, Nettie resigned herself to not knowing who the man was. "He might be following you, Ralph," she said with a chuckle.

Ralph's scowl did nothing to reassure her. As though it had never happened, he forced a smile onto his face. "Why would anyone want to follow me?" He took another mouthful of coffee, then pulled a cigarette out of his pocket, preparing to light it.

"Please, Ralph," Nettie pleaded. "The smoke affects my voice."

He nodded then and returned it to the fancy cigarette case he carried everywhere he went. "I owe you that much." They both knew if it wasn't for Nettie deciding to pursue her singing career, he wouldn't be here.

Claude Dupont, Nettie's father, set up a trust for young people down on their luck. They were set up to learn whatever it was they decided to do in life. Ralph had a talent for playing piano, and his future career was begun.

Coming from a difficult family situation, Ralph's music lessons were held at the Dupont home. That's where he and Nettie had met. It was a childhood friendship, that grew over the years.

Some years later, when Nettie decided to leave home, Ralph went with her.

Nettie yawned, and Ralph stared at her. "It's been a big day," she said. "I hate when we move to a new venue. I'd much prefer to stay in one place for a much longer time."

"Get that manager of yours to book longer gigs."

Nettie laughed. Ralph did too. If she had an manager, they wouldn't be playing in dives like this one.

Their next booking, now *that* could be lifechanging. Performing at the Royal Imperial Music Hall was a lifelong dream. How they'd even known about their show, Ivory and Melodies, Nettie would never know. The fact they were booked there was a dream come true. It gave the pair something to look forward to. It also made her wonder why they had bothered with their current booking.

Deep down she knew – first of all, they needed the money. Secondly their music hall booking wasn't for some weeks. *What were they supposed to do in between?*

Ralph ate the last of his cake and stood. "Let's go," he said, offering her his arm. Nettie pulled her shawl up around her shoulders, then they headed toward the two-bit hotel they were staying in.

She pulled two sets of keys out of her reticule as they arrived at the run-down hotel. When she'd left home, Nettie did not know she would end up in such a ramshackle establishment. The bed was barely tolerable, and the sheets threadbare. The towels were almost falling to pieces, and she could hear mice scrambling across the room as she tried to sleep. The comings and goings throughout the night told her rooms were available by the hour.

Thank goodness they only had one more night in this sleazy place. Next time she would choose their accommodations more carefully.

She handed Ralph his key. Neither of them earned quite enough to make a living, but they got by. One of these days they'd make the big time, and things would be different. It was the one thing she longed for. Not for the money. That wasn't important to her. She wanted to rub her father's face in it. To show him her talents were just that, and the fact her dreams didn't match his didn't mean they weren't worthwhile.

Ralph always waited with her while she entered her room. He liked to think he was her protector. "Ralph," she whispered as she pushed the door open, her key still in her hand. "The door was open. I know I locked it."

Suddenly, Nettie was shoved aside as a blur ran past her. She toppled over and let out a squeal.

Ralph leaned down and helped her up. "Are you hurt?" The concern on his face was heartfelt.

She brushed his worry aside. "I believe I'm still in one piece." She might have sounded fine, but she was trembling. Not surprising, given the circumstances.

"Let's check if anything is missing." Ralph was about to step into the room when she caught him by the arm.

"I'm afraid," she said, her voice quivering. "There could still be someone in there."

He stared at her then. "Of course, you're right. We'll go to the front desk and find out how to get the police here."

"And tell them what? Someone broke in, but there was little to steal? I mostly have clothes in there, as you know. There's little of value. My costume is probably the only item of value." She stared at him then, daring Ralph to disagree.

He studied her for what seemed forever, then nodded. "Well, you can't sleep there tonight," he said, dragging her away from her room.

Nettie agreed. It was the last thing she wanted – what if they had a second attempt? They near ran to the front desk, but no other rooms were available.

"You'll have to bunk in with me," Ralph said.

It wasn't an option. Nettie had a reputation to protect. Besides, Ralph's room only had one bed.

As they walked down the corridor toward his room, she was grabbed from behind. Nettie tried to scream, but a hand was forced over her mouth. Ralph flew into action to defend her.

Until a gun was shoved in his face.

"Move slowly to your room," he told Ralph, still waving the gun in his face. Nettie was petrified, and rightly so.

She had done nothing to hurt anyone, and saw no reason for this to happen. "Sit down on the bed, both of you," he demanded, then grabbed a nearby chair and sat facing them. "My name is Hank Carmichael."

Was this the man who had been stalking them? It was hard to tell, since she'd never seen his face except for two seconds tonight as they sat in the café. "What do you want?" Her words were firm, demanding.

He glanced down at the gun still in his hand, then stared at the pair sitting on the bed in front of him. "Your father sent me."

"My father? He wiped his hands of me." Nettie was certain her shock at his words would be clear.

"He was worried about you." The man looked down at the gun again. "If I put this away, do you both promised to stay where you are and listen?"

His eyes were trained on Ralph who was far more of a threat to him than Nettie. "I promise," Ralph said firmly, and Hank put the gun away. Nettie breathed a sigh of relief.

"I'm getting something out of my pocket," he said, his eyes trained on Ralph. "It's my business card." He handed it to Nettie. The card read *Hank Carmichael – Private Investigator*.

"You're a private investigator? Why would my father hire you? I'm not doing anything wrong." She was confused. Maybe he only wanted her to be safe.

"Miss Dupont," Hank said slowly. "Your father was concerned you were in danger."

Nettie considered his words carefully. "Was concerned? So I'm not in danger anymore?"

A sadness came over his face. "Your father is dead, Miss Dupont."

Nettie gasped. *This surely wasn't true? She would have heard. Wouldn't she?* "I don't believe you," she said firmly. "I would know if that happened."

She watched as he studied her. "Are you certain?" he asked gently. He reached into his pocket again.

"I have proof." Hank Carmichael unfolded a newspaper clipping and showed it to her.

"Industrialist Dead." The words blurred in front of her eyes. She wiped at the tears that rolled down her face. Nettie's head was spinning.

"My father is really dead?" A sob escaped her lips then, and she turned her head away. She wanted to run, to get away from this man who dispensed bad news by the handful.

He nodded. "I'm afraid he is. He was very concerned about your safety. It's the reason he contacted me. As his sole heir, you are now a very rich woman. He asked me to protect you, and that's exactly what I am going to do."

"None of this makes sense," she whispered. "My father cut me off. I'm not even in his will."

Hank shook his head. "He might have told you that, but it's not true. He paid me upfront to ensure I looked after you, even after…" He stopped then, and Nettie realized he was about to say, even after he was dead.

Her eyes filled with tears again.

"What can I do to help?" Ralph asked, his sadness clear. Ralph knew her father well. He'd been there when Ralph was in a precarious position. Claude Dupont was a good man and would do anything for anyone. He'd taken Ralph under his wing, and ensured he had a good life ahead of him.

"There's nothing you can do." Hank glanced from Ralph to Nettie. "First thing is to get you both out of this dump. The security here is non-existent." He thought for a moment or two. "Gather up your belongings, both of you. We need to move quickly."

"My room was broken into tonight," she explained.

"I know. They've escalated."

"You've been watching me? Was that you at each performance?" She studied Hank as he writhed under her scrutiny.

"It was not," he finally said, and her heart pounded. "I kept out of sight, but kept a keen eye on you. Each time I've just missed catching the man trying to kill you."

"They murdered my father," she said, as though only now understanding the situation. Her voice broke as she spoke the words out loud.

"Unfortunately, there is no proof of who killed your father. At least that's what the police have said."

Ralph stood, then gathered up his few belongings. They traveled light. It wasn't easy hauling a lot of belongings from town to town all the time. "I'm packed," he said shortly.

"I don't know how much of a mess they've made of my room," Nettie said, her heart still breaking over her father. "I was afraid to check once that man came running out."

"You saw him?" Worry etched his face.

Nettie studied him. "Not really. He moved so fast it was all a blur."

Hank nodded then. "Let's get your belongings, then we'll leave." They headed out to the corridor again, Hank checking it was safe first. "All clear," he said, then stepped out of Ralph's hotel room.

They went next door to Nettie's room, and she glanced about in despair. They had pulled the room to pieces, even shredding the mattress. What they'd hoped to find, she had no idea. If they thought she carried hordes of cash, they'd be wrong. She had little in her bank account since her father cut off her allowance. All she had was the money her father had previously added to her bank account, and that was surely closed to being drained by now. She and Ralph had regular bookings, but the smaller gigs did not pay so well. Nettie knew once they got the big break all performers hoped for, things would be different. She hoped the booking at the Royal Imperial Music Hall was all it was said to be.

She shoved her strewn belongings, including her costume, which was thankfully unscathed, into a carpetbag, then quickly left the room. Just being there gave her the shivers. "Where are we going?" she asked as they left the hotel.

Hank stared at her momentarily. "Somewhere far safer than this dive." He shook his head as though he couldn't believe an industrialist's daughter would stay in such a place.

"I had no choice," she told him firmly. "Father cut off my allowance, and we were surviving on a pittance."

Hank turned to face her. "Your father did not stop your allowance. He only told you that to try to change your mind. If you'd taken the time to check your account, you would know the money is there."

Despite her shock at his words, Nettie should have known. Her father had never been a cruel man, but he went to his grave believing his daughter hated him for what he'd told her. She would never hate her father. They might have disagreed on several points, but hate was never an option.

A sob left her, and she put her hands to her mouth. Claude Dupont was a good man. A kind man. He helped many people who were down on their luck, including some of his employees. He set up a foundation that ensured families were not destitute. He'd even built a small village on the outskirts of town that offered refuge to those in a desperate situation.

Her father was fully aware not everyone was as well off as he was.

Nettie felt a hand on her back. She glanced up to see it was Hank. "I promise I will keep you safe," he said. She nodded, but wasn't sure he could make a promise like that.

Hank signaled to a cab, and they all climbed in. "Take us to the Sapphire Hotel in Helena, please, driver," he commanded.

Nettie gasped. "I can't afford the Sapphire Hotel," she whispered.

Hank laughed. "To be frank, you can. You're rich. But don't worry, the cost has already been taken care of."

"Taken care of? How…"

Hank sighed, as though she should already know the answer. "Your father set up an expenses account for me to access as required. It is for all expenses occurred to keep you safe."

Nettie nodded, but she wasn't sure she truly understood. How long had Hank Carmichael been following her? It didn't sound like this was a last-minute thing. Nor did it sound as though it hadn't been meticulously planned. "I gather the Sapphire Hotel has security."

"Of course. They have a lot of celebrity and high-profile guests. No one will get past their security."

It left Nettie wondering how much danger she really was in.

Chapter Two

Hank hurried them out of the cab and into the plush hotel. He glanced about. The level of security was even higher than he envisaged, but it had to be. Their clientele were all high class, and rich. They couldn't afford to stay there otherwise.

Two men in uniforms stood at the front door. The slight bulge under their jackets alerted Hank to the fact they each carried guns. It was reassuring.

The Concierge welcomed their arrival, and Nettie blushed at the attention. Ralph glanced about, taking in every little detail. It was clear neither had ever been in such an establishment. Not that Hank spent his time in places such as this, but since he'd worked for Claude Dupont, this had become more the norm for him.

He held Nettie's carpetbag as they entered, but it was whisked out of his hands as the Concierge clicked his fingers. Ralph's bag taken from that man's grip. Hank was still uncertain about Ralph. *Would he be more of a hindrance than a help?* He only knew as much about Ralph as Claude Dupont had deemed to tell him.

From what he'd gleaned, Ralph Hanover and Nettie had been friends much of their lives. That could be a major stumbling block. Hank would not intentionally put the man in danger, but Nettie was his priority. If keeping her safe meant leaving Ralph behind, then that's exactly what he would do.

"Good morning, Sir," the Concierge said, his head held high. "How can I help you?" His eyes took in the small group, and he smiled the most fake smile Hank had ever seen.

Hank stared at him. He wasn't certain how Nettie would take this, but it had to be done. "We need two rooms," he said quickly. "A single for Mr. Hanover, and a double for my wife and myself." His heart pounded as he waited for the explosion. But it never came.

He wanted to turn and face her, but was afraid of what he would find in Nettie's expression. Her father had warned him – she was gentle as a lamb most of the time, but cross her, and she was more like the devil. The thought terrified him.

The Concierge glanced at Nettie's hands. *Had the man guessed they were not really married?* Even if he had, there was nothing Hank could do about it.

"Your keys, Sir. And yours, Mr. Hanover." Another click of the fingers and they were escorted to their rooms. Looking further, Hank saw the security was even higher than he expected. Apart from the staff you would expect in a hotel of this caliber, security guards were scattered about the lobby. If that didn't deter would be attackers, he wasn't sure what would.

They climbed the stairs behind the porter, and he risked a glance at Nettie. She was quietly fuming.

Ralph was dispensed to his single room, which, with a larger bed, would still be far bigger than anything Hank had stayed in over all his years.

Nettie's lips were pursed, and her face was wound as tight as string. Despite that, she said not a word until they were in *their* room.

He tipped the porter and sent him on his way. The moment the door closed behind him, Nettie let loose. He'd prepared himself for this, so it was really no surprise.

"How dare you? I am not some soiled dove, here for your pleasure!" No longer fuming silently, she was letting him know exactly how she felt. "We are not married. Nor would I ever marry the likes of you." She stared down her nose at him.

Claude had warned him, but he had totally discounted the older man's words. The way Nettie looked now, she was just getting warmed up.

"Furthermore…"

He interrupted her. "Your father suggested this place. I can't protect you if you're in another room." He stepped toward her, and she took a step back. "I have no intention of harming you, or for that matter," he said with a sigh, "laying a hand on you."

Was that shock he saw on her face? One moment she was bemoaning the fact he'd ordered a double room, then she is offended? It was laughable, but he dare not laugh.

He decided not to pursue the conversation and glanced around the room instead. The room was beautifully decorated, and as well as a four-poster bed, included two side tables with matching lamps, and a sofa. A married couple could cozy up on that sofa.

Of course, they wouldn't be doing that, since they weren't really married.

There was a small, round table with two chairs. Room service was available twenty-four hours a day here, according to Nettie's father, and no doubt they could eat at that table. He'd rather do that than risk taking her out in public – even if that was in the hotel's private dining-room.

"You will sleep on the sofa," she said, her words dripping like blood.

Did she think he would force himself on her? "I know. That was always the plan. It's the reason I requested a double room."

She turned away from him then and sat on the bed, bouncing slightly, no doubt trying it out. "This would be an agreeable room for newlyweds," she said, surprising him. Until she turned to face him. "Except we are not newlyweds. We are total strangers." Nettie contemplated him for the next few minutes, then pursed her lips again. "How do I even know you are who you say?" She tapped her foot on the floor impatiently, no doubt wanting him to prove his position.

"I gave you my card."

"You did," she said with a tentative smile. "Except anyone can have business cards printed. I could do the same if I wanted." She reached into her reticule and handed him one of *her* business cards. "Oh, what do you know," she said sweetly. "I did do that." She squinted as she studied him, ensuring Hank knew she wasn't convinced.

He didn't want this. He'd told Claude the whole thing was a bad idea. He desperately wanted her father to tell Nettie himself, but he would have none of it. Not that he'd been able to locate Nettie before her father was killed.

Hank watched as she flicked off her shoes and lay down on top of the bed. "I'm tired."

"Then go to bed," he said. "I'll be fine here on the sofa." He walked over to the wardrobe and pulled out two blankets and a pillow. It was a little chilly this close to Christmas, and the hotel would no doubt be heated, but one never knew what the night would bring.

"I can escort you to the bathroom whenever you are ready."

She glared at him. "I do not need an escort."

"I'm afraid you do," he said firmly.

He heard her sigh, then she put her shoes back on. Despite her resistance, she didn't complain again.

Hank awoke to find the room empty. His heart sank.

It had taken all his might to stay awake all night, but despite his best efforts, he'd fallen asleep. A man had to sleep sometime, but it was the last thing he wanted. Now he had to determine if she'd been kidnapped, which was doubtful since he was still alive, or she'd left the room to explore.

His best guess was she'd gone to visit her friend Ralph. He pulled on his pants and shoes and headed for Ralph's room. On a day of disappointments, the maid was there, making up the bed in an otherwise empty room. *That begged the question, where were they?*

Knowing full well Hank had requested she not leave her room without him, Nettie had done so. His next best guess was she was somewhere in the hotel, along with Ralph. He'd seen the fear in her eyes last night. That wasn't something you could fake. In light of that, he was almost certain she would not leave the premises.

He headed downstairs and toward the dining-room.

The head waiter met him at the door. "Good morning, Sir," the man said, coming across as very professional.

"Good morning. I'm looking for my wife and friend." Hank glanced around the room. "Ah, there they are." He headed to their table, and he saw the disgust on the headwaiter's face at not being allowed to do his job.

Hank sat heavily at the table. "What are you doing down here?" he said between grated teeth. "I told you it's dangerous."

Nettie calmly took another sip of tea, then spoke. "You are not my boss." She then went back to her tea.

Their waiter approached the table, menus in hand. "Madam, Sirs," he said, handing them each a menu.

Hank was reassured by the gleam he saw of what appeared to be a gun under the man's jacket.

Claude was right to recommend they flee to this place. Except Hank knew they couldn't stay there forever. This was a temporary fix. Where they would go next, he wasn't sure. What he knew was Ralph would be a thorn in his side. Two could move far quicker than three, and would be less conspicuous as well.

Nettie studied the menu in her hands. She glanced over the top of it to stare at him. She was far from happy, but there was nothing Hank could do about it. He wasn't happy she'd been targeted, but he would do everything in his power to keep her safe from harm.

He couldn't drag her around for the rest of her days. He had to find a way to protect her now, and in the future. It was what Claude hired him to do, and by gosh, Hank was determined to do it.

Claude Dupont had put all his trust in Hank. He'd paid him a massive lump sum, and also set up an account that would see Hank paid regularly for the rest of his days. It was the remainder of Claude Dupont's plan that bothered Hank. Duplicity was a normal part of his job, but in this case, it didn't sit well with him.

It wasn't long before their breakfasts were served. Hank desperately need the coffee that was placed in front of him. Without it, he wasn't sure how long he could stay alert. He took a long mouthful of the fortifying liquid. He almost groaned as it slivered down his throat. Whoever invented the brew was a genius. They were probably already rich by now.

The thought made him smile.

"What are you grinning about?" Nettie's sharp voice cut through his ruminations.

"Coffee." No other explanation was necessary.

She leaned forward and whispered conspiratorially. "It's the best coffee I've ever had."

Ralph agreed.

"Given how much they are likely charging for it, you would expect it to be good." Nettie frowned then. "But don't worry," Hank quickly added. "Your father has an ongoing account here. Won't cost us a cent." The moment the words were out, he realized what he'd said. He sounded callous, given Nettie had only recently become aware of her father's death.

"When did my father die?" Her words were peppered by emotion, and it cut through his heart.

There was no beating around the bush – he just had to say it. "A few weeks ago. I've been trying to locate you ever since. You moved around so much, it was hard to find you. I'd get a lead, but by the time I'd arrive, you'd just left." He studied her then. "It was beyond frustrating."

He watched as she blinked rapidly. No doubt fighting back tears. But someone with Nettie's upbringing would not allow herself to cry in public.

Ralph suddenly reached out and covered her hand with his. She glanced down at their entwined hands and smiled briefly. "You're always there for me, Ralph. Thank you," she said, her voice full of silent emotion.

She'd said little about her father's death until now, and shown little in the way of regret. It had bothered Hank. Perhaps she was in shock before. Maybe that meant the news was finally sinking in. As much as he hated to see her in pain, she needed to deal with her anguish.

Nettie swiped at a stray tear just moments before the waiter returned with their food. Hank had lost his appetite, and apparently, so had Nettie. She shoved her food around the plate. "You need to eat," Hank told her. "We don't know what today will bring. We'll stay here as long as it's feasible, but it becomes dangerous, we may need to flee at a moment's notice."

Nettie stared at him open mouthed, along with the piano man, Ralph. "You can't be serious. All these workers carry guns, as I'm certain you do. How on earth would a killer get to me here?" She waved her hands about, taking in their surroundings. "Besides, what good am I to anyone dead?"

"Have you read your father's will?" Nettie shook her head. "In the event of your father's death, the business, his money, and all assets go to you. Everything your father owned."

"There's no other family, so I still don't see the implications of killing me." Hank could tell she was upset, but Nettie kept her feelings in check.

"If only that were true." Hank took another mouthful of his bacon and eggs and swallowed it down. The food was probably the best in town, but went down like shattered glass. "I found a distant cousin. It took a while, but he's there."

He heard Nettie gasped. "Are you certain? Father told me we had no living relatives." Her face was as white as the cloth that covered the table.

"What I discovered is the cousin, Buster Macklin, is struggling. His parents died long ago. He is your Aunt Miranda's grandson. The boy was taken from his mother when he was very young. His father's parent's brought the boy up. Once he was taken, his whereabouts was unknown." Hank watched for Nettie's reaction. Her face paled. "He's been in and out of jail, and from what I've learned, he'll do anything for money. That is evident in your father's death." Hank hastened to add, "At this point, there is no proof *he* killed your father. It is all circumstantial evidence."

"So… if I'm out of the way, he gets it all?" Nettie sat there shaking her head. "Father would have helped him out, had he known of this cousin's existence."

"I came to know your father well over the last several months. I believe that to be true."

Nettie nodded. Claude Dupont was not a greedy man, and Hank was certain he would have helped if asked. Or even if he hadn't been asked and became aware of the man's existence. "Eat up. It's not a good idea to be out here for a long time." Hank continued to eat, but the others picked at their food. Ralph drank the last of his coffee and stood. Hank motioned for him to sit down again. "It's better if we move about as a group."

Ralph continued to stand, but scowled. He clearly wasn't happy. There was nothing Hank could do about that. "Enjoy the opulence of this wonderful hotel, and don't worry about anything else," he said. "Let me lead you both. And pray it all works out in the end."

Ralph suddenly sat down again. Hank would have to keep an eye on Nettie's friend.

Chapter Three

Nettie had never enjoyed opulence. It made her uncomfortable. Ralph, on the other hand was lapping it up.

He'd never been able to enjoy such luxury, the way she had. She studied Ralph as he ate dessert. She knew he had a sweet tooth, but he seemed to be really enjoying it. They'd not had the money to splash around before, so he really was taking advantage of the situation.

Not that Nettie was concerned. Her father had enough money to last a lifetime and then some.

She swallowed hard. The truth was, she had control of that money now, which was precisely why this Buster Macklin wanted her dead. From what Hank had told her, might have been unknown to the family but was still blood.

From what she'd been told, he was around Nettie's age, which made it even more surprising that her father did not know about him.

She stared down into her teacup, the pale brew mesmerizing her. "We have a performance booked in a few weeks," she said out of the blue.

Hank studied her for mere moments. "You'll have to cancel. It's far too dangerous."

"We've worked so hard to get that booking." Her voice was so quiet she hardly recognized it. "Gone are the days of begging venues to take us on. This could kill any future bookings." Even saying the words out loud, Nettie didn't want to admit the facts; better to kill bookings than for her to be killed. "The Royal Imperial Music Hall is the most prestigious booking we've ever had. It could make or break our career."

Hank stared at her with sad eyes. "I'm sorry," he said, then gulped his coffee.

Nettie pushed her dessert around the bowl. The food here was delicious. Lunch had been the best meal she'd had for a very long time. With money scarce, she and Ralph had skimped on food. They'd eaten well enough, but never indulged. Dessert was off the list of possibilities, but with Ralph's sweet tooth, she indulge him with cake here and there. It never hurt to pamper him.

Ralph stared across the room, and Nettie followed his line of vision. The Grand piano in the corner of the room stood untouched. She knew he longed to play it. After all, when would he get the chance again? Especially if Hank prevented them from attending the Royal Imperial Music Hall in San Francisco.

Ralph suddenly stood, and without a word, hurried across the hotel's private dining area, and sat at the piano. The headwaiter stared at him momentarily, then nodded. Ralph smiled. He was in his glory – this was something Nettie knew to be a wish of his from long ago. To play today, at that beautiful piano, even to people not particularly interested, would be a very special day for him indeed.

He lifted the lid and stretched his fingers. Ralph played a few notes. Nettie knew it was to ensure the piano was in tune. She'd seen him do it hundreds of times before.

Heads snapped up as he began to play. If it hadn't been for Claude Dupont, Ralph would not be playing today. It was Nettie's father who'd paid for his lessons. There was no doubt Ralph was talented. Her father had been so proud of Ralph and the work he'd put in to become as good as he was now.

She could see why her father spent his hard-earned money ensuring Ralph received the tuition he required. It warmed her heart to know her father was such a generous and caring man. It was only one reason she was adamant, had Claude Dupont know about Buster Macklin, he would have ensured his future was secured.

Knowing her father, he would have brought him to the family home. He would have clothed and fed him and given the man a generous allowance as well.

How did this person slip through the net? It had her totally bamboozled.

"He's good," Hank said, glancing about at the other guests as he listened to Ralph's playing. "No wonder you work with him."

Nettie smiled. "He is good. My father paid for his tuition, you know?" Her voice broke on that last sentence.

"I can believe it. Your father was a very generous and very caring man." He reached across and covered Nettie's hand with his. "I was down and almost out when he contacted me. If it wasn't for Claude Dupont, I would probably live in the streets right now."

Nettie raised an eyebrow at that revelation. "My father was very special," she said, and a tear rolled down her face. Hank wiped it away and squeezed her hand.

Suddenly, applause broke out. Ralph stood and bowed. He was beaming, and Nettie had never seen him so happy. The response filled her with joy – for Ralph. He deserved the accolades.

Hank glanced about. All eyes were on Ralph, which wasn't surprising. Unfortunately, he was now making his way back to their table, and soon eyes would be on Nettie. Given where they were, it shouldn't be an issue. Security was high, and the staff at the Sapphire Hotel were always fully aware of their rich guests. It was the reason Claude Dupont had suggested this place.

They would stay as long as they could, then move on. He was aware Nettie wanted to perform at their next booking, but it was not possible. Hank couldn't allow for her to be put in danger.

How was he expected to protect her when she was up on a stage? It was like telling the killer, *here I am – come and kill me.* His attention was pulled away as Ralph took his seat at their table once more.

"That was amazing," Ralph said. He turned to Hank then. "I've never had the chance to play on an instrument of that caliber before."

He was breathing heavily, which told Hank the other man was running on adrenalin. "Take a sip of water, Ralph," he said firmly. "It will make you feel better."

Nettie and Ralph both stared at him. "See how he's breathing heavily? Adrenalin has kicked in. He needs to let his body calm down." He turned to Ralph then. "Ralph, I say this with all respect – if we have to run at some point, and you're not up to it, I'm taking Nettie. If I have to leave you behind, I will."

Nettie appeared shocked and opened her mouth to speak. Ralph intervened. "I totally understand, and wouldn't have it any other way." He reached across and covered Nettie's hand. "You are the most important person here," he said firmly.

"If that happens, Ralph," Nettie said, tears dancing on her lashes. "You stay here. I will cover the costs, no matter what."

"You don't have to…"

Nettie interrupted. "No, but I want to."

Hank rolled his eyes. "This is all very cozy," he said. "But I think we should go back to our rooms. It's far safer there." He began to stand but waved the other two down. "I need to speak to the Concierge. You two wait here. I'll be back shortly."

Nettie nodded. "We'll be here when you get back." He sure hoped it was true.

He left the restaurant and headed straight to the Concierge's desk. Hank arranged for the rest of their meals to be served in their rooms. Knowing the relationship between Nettie and Ralph, he arranged for all three of their meals to come to their room.

"There's something else," Hank said, lowering his voice as much as possible and still be heard. "It needs complete discretion."

"We are renowned for our discretion," the Concierge told him. His expression one of hurt.

Hank explained the situation, and the fact Ralph may be left behind at the drop of a hat. He made arrangements for all of Ralph's charges to be billed to Claude Dupont's account, which was now Nettie's account. Hank handed over a large tip, and was met with a grin. He was assured his request would be fulfilled – without a doubt. "I will speak with the manager immediately," he said.

As he walked back to the dining-room, Hank shook his head. It was amazing what money could do for the rich and famous.

Arriving back at their table, Nettie and Ralph had their heads together. It bothered him greatly. They quickly pulled apart on seeing him approach.

"We've decided to perform at our next gig." Nettie's words were firm, and left no room for argument. Except Hank had no choice but to argue.

"Not going to happen," he said, glancing from one to the other. "I know you want to do it, but, Nettie," he said, "it's far too dangerous. We've been over this before." He sighed then. What would it take to get through to these two?

"I'm willing to take that risk." Nettie stared at him then. *Did she think her tough stance would be enough to change his mind?*

"I'm not, and that's the end of it." Hank stood then and indicated for them to follow. "We need to return to our rooms," he said. *Why did he feel like he was dealing with two young children who wanted their own way?* He not only found it frustrating, he found it particularly annoying. Especially given he was trying to keep Nettie alive.

Chapter Four

A voice called through the door at the same time a knock could be heard. "Room service."

Hank went to the door and cracked it open. He peeked around the corner of the door, checking to see it was who they said they were. he stared at the food trolley, then lifted the cloth covering the whole thing, checking there was no one under it.

When it was clear, he indicated for the waiter to enter their room.

Ralph sat staring at them both, not saying a word. Their waiter placed their food on the table then left them alone.

"That's going a bit far don't you think?" Nettie asked once the man had left.

Hank stared at her. "I have to be certain you're safe," he said as he studied her. "What if there'd been someone under there? You wouldn't think it foolish then, would you?"

Instead of answering, she rolled her eyes. "Honestly Hank, I think you've gone too far this time."

Hank rubbed his hands together. "Let's eat, I'm feeling peckish."

"It smells delicious," Nettie said, leaning into the food.

The room was then silent as they all concentrated on eating. Hank reached for his coffee, and Nettie stared at him. "What?" he demanded. He hadn't said a word – no one had, but she studied him nonetheless.

She pursed her lips and straightened her back. "Ralph and I have a firm booking in three weeks, and we're not letting our audience down."

"No," Hank said firmly.

Nettie stood her ground, and Hank could see she was determined before she even spoke. "I'm not asking, I'm telling you," she said, her gaze piercing him. "In case you've forgotten, I'm your boss now."

He wanted to slap the grin off Ralph's face right there and then, but it would do no good. "Technically, your father is my boss. He might not be here in the flesh, but he was alive when he issued his orders to me. It was also Claude Dupont who paid my retainer, and then my wages."

"Don't mince words," Nettie said, looking annoyed. "I now own the business, and I am going to that performance, and so is Ralph." She appeared more determined than ever. "I'm not discussing it with you any further."

Hank couldn't believe what he was hearing. Claude Dupont warned him about Nettie's determination, but he'd been doubtful. He should have realized it would be the case, as she'd left her father's fold to become a music hall performer – her dream job. If Mr. Dupont had his way, she would never have left his side.

It was fortunate she had, otherwise Nettie might also be dead now. Hank sat quietly fuming. If she wanted to be technical, and obviously she did, Nettie was correct — she was his boss. The contract he signed was between himself and Claude Dupont, and there was no changing that.

"We need to rehearse," Nettie suddenly said as she reached across the table and distributed the desserts.

Hank just shook his head. *Where did she think they would do that?* He'd arranged their meals to be served in here to keep her safe, but now she wanted to go out in public.

And then it hit him. Ralph's foray into playing in public had no doubt given her the idea. Hank just shook his head. It was apparent Nettie had made her mind up. At least while they were at the Sapphire Hotel, he could keep them safe. The moment they stepped outside the building, that was where Buster Macklin could, and likely would, attack her.

Apart from the dining-room, there was also a piano in the hotel's function room. Either of those places would keep her safe, but the function room would be far safer and away from prying eyes. "Alright," he said, resigned to the fact they would rehearse with or without his blessing. "I'll make arrangements for you to rehearse here." He wanted to add it didn't mean they would perform at the music hall the pair were booked at, but decided not to voice the words. That was a discussion for another time.

A slow smile crossed Nettie's lips, but she didn't utter a word.

"Thank you," Ralph said quietly. "We appreciate it."

He knew they did and nodded his acceptance. How he would keep them from leaving the hotel was another barrier he had to overcome.

The three of them sat around chatting until room service returned to collection their soiled dishes. "I need to speak to the Concierge as a matter of urgency," Hank said.

"Of course," their waiter responded, as he collected everything and placed it on his trolley.

Nettie sat with a smug look on her face. She might have won this round, but he had to dig in his heels beyond that.

Of course, the concierge was delighted to have them rehearse at the hotel. Unfortunately, the function room was fully booked for the next few days for a conference being held there, but they were welcome to rehearse in the dining-room when it was empty.

Hank knew Ralph and Nettie would be happy to perform during mealtimes, but that certainly wasn't his preference. A low profile was what he wanted. Besides, they had to eat sometime.

Nettie grabbed her fan. According to her, she couldn't rehearse dance steps without the fan, as it was an integral part of her routine. He'd never seen her perform and was curious to watch.

They walked down as a group. Hank had demanded that, although why he did, he wasn't sure. Ralph was not his responsibility, but as Nettie's friend, he felt as though he was. He'd watched the pair together, and although they had a special relationship, and an affinity of sorts, he wasn't convinced they were a couple.

He was certain Mr. Dupont would want him to look out for Ralph as well, but Nettie would always be his priority.

The door to the dining-room was blocked when they arrived, as it was being cleaned. Hank spoke to the staff there, and they were given entrance. He watched as Ralph flexed his fingers before he was even close to the piano. It was clear playing was a passion for him, not just a job.

Nettie strolled into the room, her feathery fan held close to her chest. There wasn't a lot of room at the front of the large dining-room. The area was set up with a piano and chair and little else, but the staff graciously moved some tables back for them. Ralph warmed up while they did so, playing a few scales. Nettie prepared herself with some warm up stretches. She would normally do that off stage, she told him.

Hank sat at the table near to the front. A waiter had placed a coffee in front of him, which was gratefully accepted. He watched the two interact silently up on the small stage. A signal here, and a nod there, and then began their rehearsal.

Ralph began to play, then an almost invisible nod, and Nettie came in from the side. Presumably, she would normally arrive from backstage. Her fan mostly covered her face, and she slowly lowered it down as she began to sing. Her voice was sultry.

There was no other way to explain it. He wouldn't say she exactly danced, rather she moved across the room with ease. Hank couldn't take his eyes off her.

He was totally mesmerized by their performance, and didn't want it to end. When the music stopped, the room was filled with applause. Everyone had stopped working to watch them, which was not surprising. Hank was on his feet, clapping along with everyone else. He felt moved, and could see why they'd been booked by the Royal Imperial Music Hall.

Sadly, he couldn't allow them to perform there, but he would humor them, and allow them to continue rehearsing. It was the best he could do.

"Bravo!" The clapping and voice coming from the back of the room startled Hank, and he suddenly turned, reaching for his gun, bringing it in to full view.

He heard Nettie's startled gasp, but couldn't afford to turn toward her. He must concentrate on the stranger who had spoken. "It's alright, friend," the man said. "I am Walter Gawne, manager of this wonderful establishment." He extended his hand to Hank, who wasn't convinced. Until the dining-room staff comfirmed who the man was.

Hank replaced the gun in its holster. "Apologies Mr. Gawne. I'm very pleased to meet you. Thank you for allowing Ralph and Nettie to rehearse here."

"It is our pleasure," the other man said. "It's rare we get to witness performances of such caliber. Could we entice you to perform here tonight?"

Hank frowned. *Did he not understand the level of danger Nettie was in?* "I will, of course, provide additional security for Miss Dupont," he said quietly, when he'd reached Hank's side. "I would not put her in danger."

"My wife…" Hank began. He was about to refuse his offer when Nettie interrupted.

"Yes, of course," she said, beaming. Hank groaned. She had overridden all his wishes and now accepted an offer she absolutely could have refused.

They all sat down at Hank's table and worked out the details. There would be one performance, and one only. Two security staff would stand at the back of the room, each of them armed. After the performance, the group would be escorted back to their rooms.

The added security was certainly appreciated, but he'd prefer the performance didn't happen at all.

"Well, that's all arranged," Nettie said, then leaned in and kissed him gently on the lips. "Now, dear husband," she said, raising her eyebrows, "Ralph and I need to continue rehearsing."

Before she could leave, he pulled her to him again, and kissed her. Only this kiss had far more fervor than the one she'd offered up. He quickly realized he'd done the wrong thing.

Hank's lips buzzed where her lips had touched his. Her arms slid up around him, and she whispered in his ear. "Be careful what you wish for," she said with a chuckle, then moved to the front of the room once more.

Chapter Five

The moment their lips met, Nettie knew she'd done the wrong thing.

She wanted to pay Hank back for telling the hotel staff they were married. Instead, her prank backfired. Not only had a shiver ran down her spine, but Hank looked shell-shocked. Then a brief smile played on his lips and her pulled her in and kissed her this time.

If they didn't have an audience, she wondered if she would have kissed him at all. Or if he would have pulled her close and kissed *her*.

"Are you ready?" Ralph called, bringing her back to reality. "We should take advantage of whatever time we get to rehearse."

He was right, of course he was. Time was precious. Especially now. She still hoped to convince Hank they should play at the Royal Imperial Music Hall. It was a long shot, but she had no intention of letting them down. That meant if she had to use unconventional means to get there, she would. Hank's protests would not stop her.

"Your wife is very good," Walter Gawne said, still sitting at the table.

His words made Nettie smile. It wasn't often they were complimented. Having the opportunity to play in a place of this caliber was something both she and Ralph had dreamed about for a very long time. Hank didn't want them to play in public because of the perceived danger. He didn't understand it was a lifelong dream that could easily slip between their fingers if they didn't follow through.

Ralph played another song from their repertoire, and Nettie settled herself into position, readying herself to sing. She opened her mouth, then… dropped the fan. It hit the floor quietly, and she stared down at it.

Never in all the performances she'd done had she dropped her prop. Never.

It shook her to her core. "Sorry, Ralph," she said as she bent down to pick it up, and he stopped playing. She glanced across at Hank. He mouthed *are you alright?* She nodded she was, but if she was truthful with herself, she wasn't. The reality of what had happened finally hit her. Her father's death had finally sunk in. Never again would she see him.

They'd not always seen eye to eye, but they loved each other, and that's what mattered. Now she would never hold him again. She would never talk to him again. Her heart pounded and her head spun.

Then everything went black.

Nettie's eyes fluttered open, and she glanced about. The first thing she saw was Hank's face. He was so handsome. His brown eyes stared at her, and his wavy black hair fell over his forehead. He squeezed her hand, and it felt so reassuring. "Welcome back," he whispered. Warmth flooded.

She heard murmurings somewhere nearby. "Mrs. Carmichael," a strange voice said. "I'm Doctor Spencer Franklin. You fainted. I wonder if you might be pregnant," he said, a frown on his face.

Nettie almost laughed. She would have to be truly married for that to happen. "I'm not pregnant, Doctor," she said, keeping her voice calm. She wanted to say it was all this madness going on around her, but refrained. "My…" she swallowed back the emotion that had already overtaken her. "My father recently died. It was quite a shock," she said, stating the truth. She slowly sat up then, and Hank's arm went around her back, supporting her. She enjoyed the feel of his touch, and felt reassured knowing he was there in her time of need.

"Take it slowly, and don't do too much for the rest of the day," the doctor said.

"Thank you, Doctor Franklin," Hank said. "We appreciate your help."

The doctor nodded, then left the room. Glancing over Hank's shoulder, Nettie noticed the hotel manager standing there. "We'll cancel tonight's performance," he said quietly, but Nettie didn't want to do that.

"Let's not," she blurted. "The performance is hours away. I'll rest up in the meantime, and I'm sure to be fine by tonight."

"Only if you're certain," the manager said.

"I am certain." Nettie stood then. "I apologize for causing all this commotion," she said, and she truly meant it. The last thing she wanted was to make a spectacle of herself.

"Don't be silly," Hank said, then helped her stand. They quickly returned to their room. "You should lie down for a while," he told her. "I'll arrange food while you sleep." He helped her to the bed, pulled off her shoes, then leaned in and kissed her forehead.

Nettie stared up into his eyes. She was getting far too fond of this man who was quickly becoming more than just her protector.

The knock at the door woke Nettie up from a deep sleep. Hank's quiet words to room service were reassuring – it meant he was close by. Her stomach rumble – she was hungry, but wasn't certain she could eat. All the upset earlier had her feeling out of sorts.

The doctor thinking she might be pregnant didn't help either. Of course, except for herself, Hank, and Ralph, no one else was aware they weren't really married. Nor did she want them to know. Her reputation would be ruined, and that would never do.

The more she thought about it, the more uncomfortable she felt about this sham marriage. As the new head of her father's business, she had to be even more careful. The moment room service had gone, she spoke. "Hank, I've been thinking."

He glanced across at her. "Should I be worried?" He studied her, and she almost squirmed under his gaze.

"Maybe." She tried to smile, but it was so forced, she abandoned the attempt. "Apart from the fact my reputation will be left in tatters if word got out we're not married, I worry about the reputation of my father's business." He frowned, totally oblivious to where the conversation was going. "Not that I *want* to marry you, but perhaps we should request a preacher."

His jaw dropped at the revelation. "Get m.. married?"

Was she really such a terrible person that the thought of marrying her was so terrible? She stared as he rolled his shoulders, then shook his head, as if to clear it.

"Forget I said anything." She felt the heat creep up her face at the embarrassment of it all.

"No. It might not be such a bad idea," Hank said, sitting on the side of the bed. He lifted her hand and brought it to his lips. "I've become quite fond of you over these past days."

She blinked. Did he think there was more to it? "I'm fond of you too, but that wasn't the purpose of this conversation."

He appeared to flounder, then studied her again. "You know, it might not be such a bad idea, all things considered."

"I don't understand." Nettie had no idea what he was getting at.

He grinned. "It would have a two-fold effect. It would save your reputation, and that of the business. Plus, it would remove you as sole heir of your father's business. This Buster person would have to kill the both of us to get to your father's empire."

The thought sent chills down her spine. "Kill us both?" She shivered visibly. "Perhaps it's not such a good idea after all."

He was still holding her hand, but she hadn't even realized. Until he squeezed it again, that is. Nettie felt so comfortable around Hank now, it was almost like they'd known each other forever. Much like her and Ralph.

Her thoughts were interrupted by another knock at the door. "That will be Ralph," Hank told her as he let go of her hand to open the door.

"Sit down. The food has just arrived," Hank said.

He stared at Nettie. "How are you feeling? I wonder if we should cancel tonight's performance."

"Not you too," she complained. "I'm certain I will be perfectly fine by tonight. I don't know what came over me."

The three sat down at the table. "I feel we've been neglectful," she said, reaching for Hank's hand. "We've not said grace since we arrived her. I guess things have been hectic, but we should never neglect something so important."

"You're right," Hank said, reaching for Ralph's hand as Nettie did the same. They formed a tight little circle, and Nettie closed her eyes. "Thank you, Lord, for this food, and for bringing us together. Thank you also, for bringing Hank to us, to keep us safe. A special mention for my father during this difficult time." Her voice broke on the last words, and a tear rolled down her cheek. Hank turned to Nettie and wiped her tear away.

"It will be alright," he said gently. "The police are looking for Buster Macklin. Trouble is, we don't know what he looks like." He sighed. "He has the advantage of being ghost-like. Invisible."

Nettie knew his words were true. *How did you catch someone when you did not know what he looked like?* She suddenly understood why Hank was being so vigilant.

"Ralph," Nettie said when they'd finished their meal. "Hank and I are getting married."

He grinned. "You already are," he said as he chuckled.

Hank glared at the other man. "This time it will be for real," he said firmly. "Although it will be a marriage in name only." He sighed then. "It's to protect both Nettie's reputation, and hopefully deter the killer."

Ralph looked disappointed. That seemed strange to Nettie; they had never been anything more than friends. "I see," he said, brightening up a little. *Did Ralph think that perhaps the two of them could marry down the track? Surely not.*

They sat around the table chatting about the future. According to Hank, that didn't include performing at the Royal Imperial Music Hall, but it was something she hoped to change his mind about. A knock at the door startled her. Hank opened it and let their room service server inside.

"We are in need of a preacher," Hank told the man. He received a curious look in exchange, but didn't comment. "Sometime today, if that can be arranged."

His words surprised Nettie, but Hank was right. The sooner they married, the better. If anyone discovered they were unmarried… she really didn't want to think about it.

"When did you make this decision?" Ralph demanded once they were all alone again. His voice held the tone of a man scorned. Nettie probably shouldn't have been shocked, but she was. They had been friends for many years and spent much of their spare time together. Ralph came to her father's house for lessons, and for piano practice. They had become quite close.

Despite everything Claude Dupont had done for Ralph, he didn't want Nettie to marry him. He'd even told her so. It was natural he wanted the best for his daughter, but Nettie was surprised at his bias against Ralph. He was always clean, well mannered, and respectful. He couldn't thank her father enough for his generosity, and vowed to pay him back one day. Her father refused his offer, saying that was not in line with the agreement they'd made.

Hank stared at Ralph before answering. "Earlier today. Nettie's reputation is on the line. She has enough to worry about at the moment, and doesn't need more to deal with."

She reached across the table and covered Ralph's hand. He was shaking, and she couldn't fathom why. "I'm sorry, Ralph. It was a last-minute decision on my part. I will feel better knowing Hank and I are truly married, and our pretense won't an issue."

Ralph nodded. "I can understand that. It came as a surprise, that's all." He glared at Hank for the blink of an eye, then turned to Nettie, but didn't say another word.

She sighed. "To be clear, it was my idea, not Hank's. I hate pretending we're married when we're not."

Another knock at the door interrupted the conversation yet again. Hank opened the door a crack. "Come in," he told the preacher who had arrived.

Walter Gawne, the hotel manager, also entered. "Is everything alright?" he asked, a worried look on his face.

Hank appeared slightly annoyed. He took the manager outside and closed the door, blocking Nettie and the others in the room from the conversation.

"I can be your second witness," he announced as they returned to the room.

"That would be most welcomed," the preacher said. "Are you sure you want to have the ceremony in here?" he asked, glancing around the small room.

Hank opened his mouth to answer, when the hotel manager interrupted. "There is a room downstairs that would be better suited. Why don't we go there instead?"

Nettie sent Hank and the others outside. She wanted to change into something more suitable as her wedding gown.

When she was ready, the group went downstairs, and in a matter of around ten minutes, Hank and Nettie were legally married.

Chapter Six

The dining-room was filled with guests. Word had got around Nettie and Ralph were doing a one-off performance. Hank had no doubt the manager instructed his staff to spread the word.

Many of the guests normally dined in the privacy of their rooms, but tonight, they changed their routine. As much as Hank tried to convince her to continue resting, Nettie would have none of it. In his opinion, there was no reason Ralph could not have performed alone, but Nettie would have none of it. Ralph's performance the previous night had been a hit. Hank could only imagine how tonight's performance would be received.

Hank was anxious. The one thing he didn't want anyone to know was the fact Nettie was staying there. Doing such a public performance meant it would be discussed outside this building and word would get out.

It was not conducive to keeping a low profile. He sat at the table closest to them, but in a position he could see any suspicious-looking men coming through the dining-room door. Not that it would help much – he did not know what Buster Macklin looked like.

As promised, they doubled security for tonight's performance. That, at least, eased his mind somewhat.

Guests could not keep firearms when they stayed there, and had them confiscated as they walked into the hotel. Normally guests volunteered them, and their word was accepted. Tonight, because of the circumstances, they frisked guests to ensure they had no hidden weapons. It was a compromise Walter Gawne would make to have the performance of a lifetime at his hotel.

Hank still wasn't convinced it was worth the risk. Although she was now his legal wife, Nettie insisted on overruling his decisions. She might just become the bane of his life.

Ralph and Nettie stood at the doorway to the kitchen, waiting to be introduced. Walter Gawne stepped out front and waved for everyone to be quiet. A hush went over the room. "Welcome everyone," he shouted, getting the attention of a couple of people who whispered in low tones. "We are privileged to have two wonderful performers with us tonight, and tonight only. Please welcome Miss Nettie Dupont, with Mr. Ralph Hanover on the piano." He extended his arm to indicate them both as they exited the kitchen.

Hank was surprised at the response they received. Everyone applauded loudly, more from respect than anything. As far as he could tell, their act was not well known.

Walter left the front of the dining-room and sat down next to Hank. The man was beaming. Hank was filled with warmth, proud of his wife for her magnificent talents. He only hoped she didn't faint like she had this morning.

Nettie followed Ralph out onto the small stage, and Ralph sat, flexing his fingers as he sat. She had her back to the audience, something Hank hadn't seen before. Nettie reached across and removed her fan from the top of the piano. The movement was so fluid, he barely saw it happen. Ralph nodded quickly to Nettie, the movement almost invisible, and began to play.

Suddenly the room was electric. She twisted to face the audience, and applause began once again.

Nettie's eyes scanned the room, taking in her audience, then she began to sing, slowly sliding the feathery fan down her face, down her chest, but covering the top of her bosom, and that was where it stayed. Now and then she fluttered the fan as she sang. Nettie took a few steps here and there across the stage, then finally stepped down into the audience.

Hank gasped. This was not part of their agreement. He began to stand, but thought better of it. "She's well protected," Walter whispered. "Nothing to be concerned about."

Nettie moved from table to table. Watching this performance, he understood now why Claude Dupont believed her to be performing burlesque, but knew that assessment to be wrong. He stared as her fingers mussed up the hair of some men in the audience. Hank fumed. He'd never been a jealous man, but he didn't appreciate his wife touching other men. And certainly not in the manner she was doing right now.

Calm down, he told himself. *It's even not a proper marriage.*

But he couldn't calm down. Despite knowing her for only matter of days, he was very protective of his wife. Of course, that's what he'd been employed to do, but there was more to it, and he knew it.

His eyes watched her every move until finally she made her way back to the stage. Hank couldn't believe how relieved he felt.

The moment the music stopped, applause broke out. She gestured to Ralph, and the applause began again. Nettie bowed, along with Ralph.

Then he sat once again, flexing his fingers as he had earlier. This time, Nettie placed the fan back on the top of the piano, and the music began again. This song was not sultry like the last one, and he was grateful. He knew it was all an act, but he didn't like to see his wife portrayed in this way.

She stayed on the stage for the entire song. When the song ended, applause broke out again. She was beaming. "Thank you, everyone. We're going to take a brief break," she said once the applause died down. "We'll be back shortly."

The pair went to Hank's table and sat down. There was a glass of water waiting for them both, as Nettie had requested. She began sipping it almost immediately.

"You two are brilliant," Walter said. Hank had never seen him so happy. "I thought you were good at rehearsal, but you're even better tonight."

"We're good alright," Nettie said, as she smiled. "I only wish father had seen us perform."

Hank stared at her then. "Your father watched you perform. He told me so."

Nettie seemed shocked. "He did? I didn't know. I wish he'd told me."

"It was in Billings, I believe." Hank tapped his forehead. "Yes, I'm almost certain that's what he said."

Nettie took another sip of water. "I'm glad," she said, then stood. Ralph followed her lead. As the pair headed toward the stage, applause broke out again. From what they'd told him previously, this was probably one of the best responses they'd had out of all the places they'd performed.

He sat mesmerized for the remainder of the performance. When they finished, the pair received a standing ovation from their audience. No one wanted it to end, and by the look on his face, Walter Gawne was amongst those who wished they could stay longer. True to his word, Walter had two men escort the group to their room. He followed along.

"That was absolutely brilliant," Walter said, still quite animated. "I wish I could convince you to perform again tomorrow night."

Hank was frustrated. They had an agreement, and now Walter wanted to entice Nettie further. "Apart from the fact you told your guests this was a one-off opportunity, you know my wife is unwell. The last thing we want is to have her fainting again."

"Of course. You are right. I apologize. Thank you again for your absolutely incredible performance. Both of you," he said, then left them alone.

Nettie was exhausted. Hank didn't have to be told to know it. "Why don't you rest for a while?" he said, guiding her to the bed.

Ralph was still in the room and took that as a cue to leave. "Hank's right. You look tired. I'll see you both later."

Hank saw him to the door, then returned to his wife. Nettie sat on the edge of the bed where Hank had left her. She appeared to be far too tired to even position herself to sleep. "Lay down," he said, as he helped her, and lay her head on the pillow. Then he removed her shoes. Nettie watched his every move despite her tiredness, and finally closed her eyes the moment her feet were free of her shoes.

He knew he shouldn't, but Hank stood over her, staring at her feet. They were married, so there was absolutely nothing wrong or immoral with him doing that. So why did he feel so guilty about his actions?

Theirs was a marriage in name only. Which meant he had no right to stare. She still wore the stockings that were hidden under her skirts, so it wasn't even as though her feet were bare.

In some ways, he understood Nettie demanding the marriage was in name only, but what if things changed? Would she still insist on keeping it that way?

Hank shook his head. Why was he even thinking this way? They'd made a decision, and that was the end of it. Nettie was far above him in status. She was rich, and he wasn't. He wasn't even suited to her. She was so easygoing and carefree – and he was the total opposite.

Ralph was more like the sort of man she would be attracted to.

He thought for a moment. *If that was truly the case, why did she kiss him earlier today?*

That was easy. He'd told a colossal lie about them being married, and she wanted to get him back. Make him pay for his sins.

Of course she did. It was the sort of thing her father warned him about. She could be cunning when it suited her. Claude Dupont had told him so. He'd been proven right.

Nettie had paid him back by marrying him.

Chapter Seven

There was a light tap on the door, and Nettie slid silently out of bed.

She glanced across the room, and in the early morning light, confirmed Hank was sound asleep on the sofa, still under the blankets. She felt bad for deceiving him, but she and Ralph had a booking. If they missed it, that would be their last performance ever.

They still had plenty of time, but they needed to be there in plenty of time. It would never do to miss their performance date. Besides, if they didn't make it with this attempt, there was still time to try again.

Word got around quickly in this business. They would be black-banned by every decent music hall in the county, if not the state if they didn't turn up to perform. Nettie was convinced even the small venues would wipe their hands of them if they were a no-show.

If only Hank had agreed to let them perform. Not that she expected the danger was as severe as he'd portrayed it.

She sighed, then slapped a hand to her mouth. Nettie needed to keep as silent as a mouse.

She didn't have many possessions, but had packed her bag earlier, when Hank was outside the room talking to the manager. It was thrown together quickly to hide her plans, but she'd managed to fold her costume in such a way it wasn't damaged. The fan was especially important, and when not in use, sat in it's own specially made carry bag for protection.

Nettie silently slipped her shoes on, then pulled her coat and bags from the wardrobe. Ralph would be outside waiting, and then they would leave. By the time Hank discovered them missing, it would be too late for him to do anything about it.

She opened the door noiselessly, ensuring Hank wasn't woken, but whether she could close it as quietly, she wasn't sure. Ralph took her bags as she endeavored to complete the task.

They both held their breath until the door was completely closed, then the pair ran.

Nettie's heart pounded, and when they arrived at the bottom of the stairs, Ralph turned to her. "Are you sure you want to do this?"

She felt bad about leaving Hank behind like this, but it had to be done. *Was she sure they should run in the night like escaped convicts?* Nettie was convinced it was the only way. "I'm sure," she said firmly, despite her misgivings. "Let's go."

They reached the front entrance, where two burly men with guns stood guarding their escape. "I'm sorry, Mrs. Carmichael. We have orders to keep you here. Mr. Hanover is free to leave if he wishes."

Nettie glanced up at the men. Her eyes going from one to the other. "You can't be serious."

"I'm afraid they are our orders. You'll have to take it up with your husband."

She was furious. *How dare Hank do this?* It wasn't even as though theirs was a genuine marriage. Besides, she was paying the bills. It wasn't even his money.

Instead of arguing, since she knew it was pointless, she strutted over to one of the sofas in the lobby. Ralph followed close behind her. "What do we do now?" he asked, shock clear on his face.

Nettie gazed at him for long moments. "Your guess is as good as mine." She glanced around the lobby. "Could we get out through the kitchen?" She raised her eyebrows, knowing it was a long shot. "I mean, we were in there the day of our performance. Did you see a back entrance?"

Ralph stared at her incredulously. "I wasn't looking, but do you truly want to steal out of here like a thief in the night?"

"Isn't that what we were trying to do?" Her head thudded. Their plan was in disarray, and now Hank would not trust either of them to do the right thing. It would result in there being no more opportunities to leave.

Hank's voice suddenly caught her attention. "Nettie!" He hollered across the room. Her head shot up, and she sunk down on the luxurious sofa in embarrassment. Ralph shuffled over, allowing Hank to sit next to her. *You skunk,* she felt like telling Ralph, but refrained. She knew in her heart Ralph had her best interest at heart. So did Hank, for that matter.

He reached for her hand and brought it to his lips. "I was terrified," he said, almost breathlessly. "I've been running around everywhere looking for you." She stared at him then. *Looking where?* As though he could read her thoughts, he answered. "I thought you might have had an early bath. But you clearly weren't there."

She almost chuckled, but thought better of it, and refrained. "I told you we had a booking." She glared at him then, but it didn't seem to faze Hank one bit.

He took a deep breath and closed his eyes, letting his breath out slowly. Like he was dealing with an annoying child. "We talked about this," he whispered. "It is far too dangerous."

"Yes, we did," she said, leaning closer to him as she spoke. "I could ask the manager to call the police for me."

Hank laughed so loudly the security people turned to face them. "You're funny. Besides, the police are fully aware of the situation. There's nothing to report," he whispered. Suddenly, his expression was not one of mirth. He was deadly serious.

Nettie had to catch her breath. Suddenly, she wasn't so sure about this man who claimed to have been employed by her father. *Was Hank Carmichael who he claimed to be? Or was he a gold digger after her inheritance?* If he was, he already had access to her money. In fact, he could claim it all for himself right now. Everything changed the moment they married.

Who was to say Hank wasn't the one who killed her father? She wondered if Buster Macklin even existed. Panic began to bubbling up in her chest. Her throat felt as though it was closing over, and Nettie stood, wanting to get away.

The moment she did, she collapsed on the floor, right there in front of everyone to see.

"Are you certain your wife is not pregnant?" Doctor Franklin asked. "Fainting is often a clear indication of the condition."

Hank stared at the doctor. "I'm as positive as I can be." He glared at Ralph then. Nettie was furious. Was he secretly accusing her and Ralph of… She wanted to slap the man senseless. It took all her effort to refrain.

"I think I've been overdoing things, Doctor," she said sweetly. "I work long hours when I have bookings."

He lifted her hand and checked her pulse. "Your heart is slowing back to a normal rate. Luckily, your husband was nearby when it happened." He snapped his medical bag closed, then turned toward Hank. "Your wife must rest. No more rehearsing or performances until she is fully recovered."

"I give you my word, Doctor," Hank said firmly.

Nettie was fuming. Again. *How dare these men make decisions about her wellbeing without her input? How dare Hank pretend he had control over her?*

The unfortunate truth was, he did have control over her. Complete and utter control, including her father's millions. And it was all her fault. It was Nettie who suggested they marry. She was the one worried about her reputation. She thought Hank was someone to be trusted. He'd made her believe her father trusted him. Now she wasn't so sure.

A tear escaped and she tried to hide her tears.

"Now, now, Mrs. Carmichael," Doctor Franklin said, patting her hand. "It might seem overwhelming right now, but things will get far better with rest." He glanced across at Hank momentarily, then turned back to Nettie. "And if you are with child, it won't be long before you'll be cradling a tiny babe in your arms." He left them alone then.

Nettie wanted to scream. "This is all your fault," she snarled at Hank.

He grinned. "According to the doctor, it is." She could easily slap that smile off his face, but luckily for Hank, they were in the middle of the lobby where she'd fainted, and were surrounded by concerned staff.

Nettie clenched her teeth. "What happens now?" she whispered, when what she really wanted to do was scream.

"When you're up to it, I'll take you back to our room to rest." He waved to the Concierge and arranged for breakfast to be brought up to their room. Ralph, he said, would eat breakfast in his own room this morning.

Was that Hank's first step toward keeping her and Ralph apart? Would she never get out of her husband's clutches? Father always said when she married, they would arrange a prenuptial to ensure her inheritance was safe. It was now too late to take his advice.

"I don't know why you continue to worry about performing at the Royal Imperial Music Hall. It's not that big of a deal." He shrugged his shoulders then, and fury boiled up inside Nettie.

"Not a big deal? Do you honestly have any idea? It's a stepping stone to the best venues in the country." She pierced him with her gaze. "But no, it's not a big deal." Today had not gone the way she'd planned.

Ralph and Nettie should be almost halfway to their destination by now. They should have been on the train that would take them to a new level in their career. Ralph definitely deserved it. He'd worked hard for many years, thanks to her father's generosity.

Nettie had also worked hard. She'd taken singing lessons and taken dance lessons too. Father had indulged her, thinking they were simply whims. He did not know she'd planned a career on the stage. She dare not tell him for fear he'd say no.

Father… was he really dead, or had Hank made that up too? Her heart suddenly lifted. Perhaps this was all an elaborate lie. If Hank had lied about the alleged cousin, Buster Macklin, then perhaps he'd lied about her father dying.

"Nettie? You've gone as white as a ghost. Perhaps you need to lie down for bit." He reached out and touched her arm. Nettie flinched. She didn't want this gold-digger touching her. He only wanted her for her money. And now he was isolating her away from Ralph, which meant she had no way to warn him.

She could see the writing on the wall. From this moment on, Hank would ensure the two were kept apart. If that were to come to fruition, it would prove her right. If it didn't, she still may not be wrong. It was hard to keep an open mind when she had become all but a prisoner to her husband.

Nettie tried to hold back a sigh, but failed. Being truthful with herself meant admitting she truly was a prisoner. Otherwise, what was that about downstairs? She was openly told her husband had ordered security to keep her there – to not allow her leave the premises.

What have I done, Father? Her silent prayer didn't make Nettie feel any better; she felt far, far worse admitting she was fooled by a petty thief.

So he might not be a petty thief, she'd admit that. But whatever he was, Hank Carmichael was clever. He had her fooled from the start. Somehow, he'd made her think their marriage was her idea.

Of course it was, but somehow he'd fooled her into asking him to marry her. To protect her reputation. And of course he'd played his cards right, pretending he didn't want to do it, when that was his goal all along. How could she have let herself be played like that? Now her father's entire fortune was at his fingertips.

It was then a thought occurred to her. She needed to verify her father's death. If he was indeed still alive, she would have no access to his vast fortune. "I need to see a lawyer," she blurted out.

The look on Hank's face was one of astonishment. "A lawyer? What on earth for?" *He would say that, wouldn't he?* Her husband wouldn't want anyone meddling with her father's bank accounts for fear she would discover he was still alive.

"Well, for starters, I need to arrange for the business to be transferred into my name."

Hank frowned. "That's already been taken care of."

"My signature needs to be lodged at the bank."

He looked even more concerned now. "You did that some years ago. Your signature is already lodged and validated. Your father asked me to ensure every necessary procedure had been dealt with. He knew his life was in danger."

"And yet no one told me," she wailed, tears rolling down her cheeks. Nettie swiped at her face, almost slapping herself for her stupidity at letting this stranger into her life.

"Nettie," Hank said, his voice almost a whisper. "I spent months trying to find you. I'd almost catch up, only to discover I'd just missed you. It was frustrating, to say the least."

He stood then and came around to where she sat at the table. Hank wrapped her in his powerful arms, and for a moment there, she forgot he was her tormenter. She leaned into him, and felt comforted, protected.

How could she have fallen for him? Hank was nothing more than a sophisticated criminal. A conman, no less. Her father taught her better than that. Yet, all it took was for her to let her guard down. The moment Hank told Nettie her father was dead, she lost her head. She was thinking with her heart, and Father taught her to never do that. Thinking with your heart was only for love, he would say. The pity of it was, she was certain she was in love with Hank.

Now she only felt hatred toward him.

Chapter Eight

That last fainting episode had left Nettie out of sorts. Hank could tell almost the moment she came around. She had near snarled at the doctor, and she did snarl at him. He still hadn't got over that. Claude Dupont told him she had a temper, but he said she was a well-mannered and caring person.

He'd seen that side of her, and now he'd seen another.

Something was bothering her, but Hank couldn't fathom what. *Had he gone too far demanding she was kept inside the hotel?* It was for her own safety. He was certain she'd planned something with Ralph. He'd seen them with their heads together occasionally, and it had bothered him. The last thing Hank wanted was for any harm to come to his wife.

His wife. He was still trying to get used to saying that. Never in his life did he expect someone like Nettie to want to marry someone like him. She was a well-educated, refined young woman. He was rough around the edges and was the first to admit it.

He wore a suit because Claude Dupont insisted on it. His employer had even paid for it, knowing Hank couldn't afford it. His assistant had sought Hank out. Mr. Dupont had seen his insignificant advertisement in the newspaper. It was a great shock to Hank.

His office was in the poor part of town, in a rundown office building. Most months he barely covered the rent and was on the verge of giving up when he received the news Mr. Dupont wanted to see him.

"I've employed a few others to find my daughter," he said. "Those fools only took my money." He harrumphed then. "Or perhaps I was the fool," the old man had told him.

Hank never set foot in that rundown building again. He worked for Mr. Dupont full-time, searching for his daughter. He was relieved to eventually catch up with her, even if it was too late to tell him employer.

Now, though, they were married. He was still rather shocked by the turn of events. Not that anyone seeing them together would know they were married. Plus, she still made him sleep on the sofa.

The bed would be far more comfortable, and more to his liking. That thought made him smile.

"Hank," her suddenly tiny voice came out of nowhere. His arms were still wrapped around her, and he had no thought of moving. It felt nice. "Why are you doing this?"

Doing what? Holding Nettie to comfort her? He was more than a little puzzled. He glanced down at her face. "I'm not sure what you mean," he said, pulling Nettie to her feet and holding her close. He breathed in her fragrance. He'd seen her dab the expensive rose perfume behind her ears. A gift from her father, she'd told him.

"If it's my money you want, take it."

Hank froze. *Her money? What on earth was she talking about?* He pushed back and studied her. "What? Your money?"

"I know my father is still alive. Where is he?"

Hank became more puzzled by the second. "Nettie," he said, holding her by the shoulders, wanting to shake some sense into her. "What are you babbling on about? I told you already, Nettie, your father is dead. I believe he was murdered by Buster Macklin." He led her toward the sofa then. "Can I get you something? Water, or perhaps you need a shot of brandy. You're not making any sense."

She shook her head vigorously. "I… I am quite confused. I can't think straight," she said. "I need proof my father is dead." She stared into his eyes then, tears dancing on her eyelashes. "I don't… I'm not convinced he's really dead."

Hank couldn't believe what he was hearing. But perhaps Nettie was in shock. Yes, that's what it had to be.

Her father's death had finally sunk in, and she was having trouble dealing with it. As you'd expect when she hadn't been able to see him and verify that for herself. He'd expected her to ask for proof well before this. A newspaper article was not exactly proof.

"I have a copy of his death certificate, if that helps," he said gently. Hank wondered if they would need the doctor again. It was now clear that's what her earlier fainting spell was about. Heaven forbid he even think it, but unless some hanky-panky was going on between Nettie and Ralph, there was no way she was pregnant. She wouldn't even let *him* sleep in the same bed as her, although they'd legally married. With a preacher, and in front of witnesses.

He sighed then. Claude Dupont said she was a delicate flower, even if she tried to appear otherwise. Her father was right. Nettie's demeanor right now was proving his point.

Nettie nodded, and Hank reached for his jacket. His hand slid into the hidden pocket inside his jacket. Her eyes watched his every move. She cringed as though he was going to… Hank gasped. *Did she think he was going to shoot her? What had come over his wife since yesterday?* Something was clearly amiss.

Hank opened the folded paper carefully and handed it to the tortured soul sitting next to him.

Lips pursed, she read the document from top to bottom, then folded it and handed it back. He turned to return his jacket to its rightful place. When he faced her again, Nettie had her hands on her face. Her sobbing cut right through his heart.

He sat down gently and cradled her in his arms. *Why did she think he'd lied to her?*

His hands stilled. Everything had changed since this morning. Since his demands saw her detained inside the hotel. "Nettie?" he whispered. His fingers under her chin, he tilted her face to look at him. "What are you thinking?" Whatever it was, it wasn't good, he was certain.

"That you…" she stopped and wiped at her tears. The tears he should be brushing aside. "Did you kill my father?" she blurted out.

Hank stared at her in disbelief. *Did his wife really just ask him that?* He wasn't sure where they went from there.

He continued to hold her as he thought about how to respond.

Hank took a deep breath and let it out slowly. Never in all his years as a private investigator had he come across such a dire situation. But neither had he been in such a position before. Claude Dupont demanded Hank look after his little girl, especially after Mr. Dupont's demise. He paid Hank wisely for his time – far too much if you asked Hank – but it got him out of a difficult situation. He'd made a promise, and Hank fully intended to keep it.

"Your father trusted me, but clearly you don't." It wasn't a question. He had no doubt Nettie had run several scenarios through her addled mind. Nothing seemed amiss until he'd had her detained. It kept coming back to that moment. Until then, she was in control.

Mostly anyway.

Once he'd taken that control out of her hands, everything changed. It was Nettie who decided to perform in the dining-room. It was Nettie who insisted on them marrying. It was also Nettie who decided she must, under all circumstances, perform at the Royal Imperial Music Hall.

And that was the point of change. If he hadn't insisted she must stay in the hotel no matter what, she would be roaming around goodness knew where right now. Both she and Ralph would be on their quest, blissfully unaware of the dangers they faced.

Even now, Hank was convinced she didn't understand the severity of her circumstances. There was only one thing for it – and he needed to do it quickly, before things got even further out of control.

His arms slipped off from around her, and he opened the wardrobe. Hank pulled out his satchel and opened it. Nettie cringed in the corner of the sofa. To allay her fears further, he dragged his hand out slowly.

She gasped. "Don't kill me!" she screamed as she turned deathly white.

Hank didn't think he could be any more shocked than he was already. "Kill you?" He showed Nettie his hands, and the papers he held there. "What I'm doing is getting out the proof I found for your father. I have no intention of harming you, Nettie. My job, my objective, it to protect you. It's what I was employed to do." No one warned Hank he might fall in love along the way.

He shook himself mentally. He had no idea where the thought came from. They were virtual strangers, linked only by the danger Nettie was in. *So why did he want to hold her for all eternity? Feel his lips on hers again?*

Hank placed the wad of papers on the table. "Look at these. It documents the investigation I undertook at your father's request, and the information I uncovered." Nettie gasped at the pile of papers in front of her. "There are many months of work here. I promise you," he said, running a hand over her back, trying to comfort her, "this is all true, genuine. I will not harm you."

Nettie stared down at the notes he'd written, and the family tree he'd drawn up. "Here," he said. "This is where Buster Macklin belongs. He is your father's deceased sister's child."

"Aunt Miranda's grandson? So he is truly an heir to my father's empire?" She closed her eyes then, and Hank wasn't sure if she was trying to take it all in, or was praying for strength. He figured she needed both.

"With your father gone, you are the sole heir." It was harsh, but had to be said.

She turned and stared at him then. "You are also an heir to my father's fortune – now that we're married."

He was, but only of Nettie's doing. It was never part of the plan. Not Hank's or Claude Dupont's. It wasn't something Claude Dupont even suggested. Hank doubted it had crossed his mind.

"We can have the marriage annulled, if that's what you want." He let his words hang in the air as he packed all his paperwork away again, but not before showing Nettie there was nothing else in his satchel.

She opened her mouth to speak, then slammed it shut again as a knock came to the door. "That's probably Ralph," she breathed. "I don't want to see him right now. I'm a mess."

He nodded, then opened the door a crack. "I want to see Nettie," Ralph demanded. Hank didn't know he had it in him.

"She's unwell and needs to rest." He tried to close the door, but Ralph jammed his foot in it, preventing its closure.

"I demand to see her. I want to ensure she is unwell, as you say." Hank appreciated the other man looking out for his friend. What he didn't appreciate was the forcefulness in which he tried to do it.

"I said no." Hank tried again to shove the door closed, to no avail.

Nettie called out then. "I don't want to see anyone right now, Ralph. I am feeling rather unwell."

Hank appreciated her words, but didn't need her intervention. Ralph needed to understand he wasn't always welcome.

"You harm a hair on her head, I'll come for you," Ralph said under his breath.

Hank was far too shocked to respond, and quickly closed the door, then locked it.

Chapter Nine

"How well do you know Ralph?"

Hank's words confused her. "I've know him since we were both teenagers. Why?"

She studied her husband as he appeared to war with himself. His expression went from shocked to curious in a matter of seconds. "He just threatened me."

Nettie laughed. "Ralph threatened you? I think you misunderstood." She shook her head then.

"How did you meet?" Hank was asking far too many questions about her friend. A friend Nettie felt she'd know forever.

"One of my father's charities. Ralph was chosen out of several candidates." She stared at him curiously. "You surely don't think Ralph is involved in any of this?"

He stared at her, his expression one of concern.

"You do!" *How could her friend of over ten years be involved in a plot to kill her?* It wasn't feasible, and Nettie would have none of it. Then her heart thudded. *Hadn't she accused Hank of something similar?* She didn't know him well enough to have the facts, and now Hank was in the same situation. "If Ralph was involved, his plan must have been hatched years ago, when he was barely a teenager. Besides, didn't you say my long-lost cousin was named Buster?" She shook her head in disbelief.

"Then why did he threaten me?"

She blinked. *Did Ralph really threaten her husband?* "Exactly what did he say?"

Hank thought hard before answering. "*You harm a hair on her head, I'll come for you.* I think they were his words. Close to that, anyway." He watched as she took it all in.

Nettie smiled. "That sounds like Ralph. He's looked out for me for as long as I can remember." She waved a hand in the air then, brushing his concerns aside.

"I can check up on him."

The smile left her face. "I know you can. Perhaps you should, if only to appease yourself. Ralph would never harm me – it's not in his nature."

"He's in love with you." Hank grimaced at his words, and it left Nettie wondering if that was because he was concerned about her safety around her friend. *Or was it because he was jealous?*

"You're being ridiculous now." She shook her head and flounced over to the sofa where she lay down.

"I'm getting a headache," she said, waving him away. But Hank didn't go anywhere. *How could he?* She'd take the entire sofa and refused to allow him on the bed. She couldn't expect him to sit at the table for long. The chairs were far too uncomfortable.

The more she thought, the worse her head hurt. Finally, Nettie closed her eyes and tried to sleep. She heard shuffling across the room, but refused to open her eyes again. She needed to sleep, and that's what she was going to do.

It wasn't long before she heard light snoring. *Where was Hank sleeping?* Not on her bed, she hoped! Nettie had banned him from the bed. It was her domain, and she'd warned him to keep away from it.

Her eyes fluttered open, and she glanced across the room toward the four-poster bed with its beautiful covering. There, on *her* bed, lay Hank Carmichael. Fury worked its way up through her. If she wasn't a lady, she would have a few choice words to say. Father would not be impressed with what she was thinking right now. And would be even less impressed if she voiced her thoughts.

She strutted over to the bed and sat on the edge, removing her shoes. She glanced across at the intruder on her bed. "I thought you were supposed to be protecting me?" she whispered, but Hank didn't move as she thought he would. Instead of wasting her breath further, she lay down on the bed, watching him the entire time.

Hank continued to snore softly, and it was beginning to irritate her. "I should call the manager," she muttered, a little louder this time.

This time, his eyes opened to stare at her. "You think so, do you?" he said teasingly, and Nettie wondered if he'd even been asleep. He half sat and leaned over the top of her, his eyes on her lips the entire time.

"What are you doing on my bed?" she asked, fully annoyed by now.

"Do you mean our bed?" He leaned in then, and gently kissed her lips.

Nettie didn't move. She wasn't sure how she felt about this turn of events. He might be her legal husband, but at no point did she give him permission to kiss her. Then she froze. Nettie started the ball rolling when she kissed him in the dining-room. It was meant to be a display of affection. To prove to those around them, they were really married.

At that point, they weren't, and it was all for show. Now they were totally alone, and she stared up into his eyes as Hank hovered above her. The next move was totally up to her. If she kissed him back, she would be signalling her assent. If she didn't, it was a totally different story. For both of them.

Nettie stared up into his big brown eyes. *How could she resist those puppy dog eyes? Did she even want to?* Hank's hand came down and brushed the hair off her face. His fingers caressed her cheek. He didn't try to coerce her either way.

And suddenly he turned away. "Hank," she whispered, and he turned back to face her. Nettie's heart pounded. *Was this a decision she would regret the rest of her life?* She stared up at him again, then pulled him toward her and kissed him.

Nettie awoke to the pounding on the door. She was still half asleep, but Hank jumped out of the bed and grabbed his gun on his way there. Nettie gasped at the sight of it. Of course, she knew Hank had a gun, and she'd seen it that first day. He'd kept it hidden from her ever since.

"What do you want?" Hank asked, his irritation clear in his voice.

"What have you done?" Ralph's voice held fury, and Nettie wondered what was wrong with him. "You filthy piece of…" Suddenly Hank flew backwards, no doubt from Ralph's fist. She knew he had a temper, but she hadn't seen it for many years. Her father had got him out of that terrible habit.

"Ralph!" she screamed. "It was my choice. Leave my husband alone."

Hank lay on the floor in only his drawers. If it wasn't so serious, it would be laughable seeing these two men fighting over her.

Ralph's head shot up. "You willingly slept with this… this…"

"For goodness' sakes, Ralph. We're married. What we do is not your business. Now apologize to Hank and get out."

Ralph glared at Hank, then stormed out. No apology was forthcoming. Once he was gone and the door was closed, Nettie hurried over to Hank. "I'm sorry. Are you hurt?" She stared at the trickle of blood coming from the side of his mouth.

Hank stared at her. It was then Nettie realized she left little to the imagination in her current attire, and reached for her robe. A slow smile crossed her husband's face. He quickly stood and locked the door, then lifted her into his arms. He held Nettie against himself for the longest time, then dropped her onto the bed. "Perhaps we should have asked for the honeymoon suite," he whispered.

Nettie thought perhaps he was right.

Ralph mostly left them alone over the next few days. He had most of his meals in his own room, and those he didn't, would be eaten in the dining-room. Nettie knew he would have spent time playing that beautiful piano. Not only did he enjoy it, Ralph had told her on many an occasions it was a way for him to get his frustrations out of his system.

Hank was taking her to the dining-room for supper tonight. He'd made it very clear to management she would not be performing, despite feeling much better after the few days of rest she'd undertaken.

It was all Nettie could do not to smile when he uttered those words.

She put on her best dress and fixed her hair to perfection. The pair went down the stairs together. Hank wore his suit and a clean shirt. Much to her disgust, he also wore his gun and holster under his jacket.

They halted at the entrance to the dining-room. "Good evening, Mr. and Mrs. Carmichael," the headwaiter told them both. "Will you be joining Mr. Hanover?" He indicated to where Ralph sat alone, near to the front.

Hank stared at her. *Did they want to join Ralph?* She guessed it would look strange if they didn't. "Thank you, yes," Nettie said. "Assuming Mr. Hanover is happy to share with us."

Their waiter smiled. His expression was one of amusement. He seemed to think Ralph would never refuse them. Perhaps that may have been the case some days ago, but things had changed between them. Ralph no longer behaved like the Ralph Hanover she'd know since her teenage years.

She watched as the headwaiter walked over to the man she once called her best friend. His head shot up, and he stared across the room at the pair. Nettie held her breath as she waited for his response. Ralph nodded and threw her a tentative smile. Nettie slowly exhaled.

Hank squeezed her hand as the headwaiter returned.

"Mr. Hanover would be pleased to welcome you at his table. Follow me," he said as he lead the way.

Despite being used to living the life of luxury as a young girl, Nettie couldn't get used to the extravagant treatment they received here at the Sapphire Hotel. She could certainly get used to it. But it wasn't the life she'd lived for the past years and knew it wasn't the way Hank had lived either.

She would have to think long and hard about their future.

"Hello, Ralph," she said as her chair was pulled out. "Thank you for the invitation."

He threw her a look that said *I didn't invite you – you invited yourself!* She would let that pass.

"Ralph," Hank said curtly. She expected nothing less from Ralph to her husband, but not the other way around. They didn't look directly at each other, and she was becoming annoyed.

"Oh, for goodness' sake, you two! This is ridiculous. Ralph," Nettie told her friend. "Hank and I are married. What we do in private is totally our business." She reached across the table and squeezed Ralph's hand. "We've been friends a very long time. We both knew the day would come when one or both of us would fall in love and marry someone else."

"Except you're not in love with him." Ralph nodded Hank's way, and Nettie sighed.

She dropped her voice even lower. "The thing is, Ralph, I am in love with him."

Hank stared at her then. A slow smile played on his lips, and her heart fluttered. How could she fall in love with someone she barely knew? Father told her it would happen one day. She was willing to bet he didn't know it would be to a man he'd employed to find her.

"Can we just all be friends? Get back to how things were before?"

Ralph reached out and covered her hand. "Of course," he said. "You are right. You're married, and what you do is not my business." He extended his hand to Hank, and the two men shook hands. Nettie couldn't have been more relieved if she tried.

"I see they've been decorating in here," she said, glancing around the room. "Don't you love December, with all the Christmas decorations? Soon it will be quite chilly and we'll be in our winter coats." She glanced out the window. No snow yet, but it wouldn't be long. Not that Nettie anticipated spending much time in the snow – not the way things were at the moment. *If the police didn't find Buster Macklin, would she ever go outside again?* Not if Hank had his way.

"If you'd been out of your room the past days, you would have seen it earlier." Ralph grinned then, which surprised Nettie. He was actually joking about the pair locking themselves away for their *honeymoon.*

It had to be a step in the right direction, surely?

Instead of answering, Hank asked a question. "What have you been doing with yourself?"

"I've played here a few times, and I've met someone."

Hank raised his eyebrows. "Met someone? Here?"

Ralph grinned. "She's a guest here at the hotel. We've been out twice, and we like each other. A lot." He turned to Nettie then. "I had to fill in my days somehow. We're planning to go to the theater one day soon."

Nettie was pleased. Ralph was her friend and deserved to be happy. "Ah, here she is now." He stood and a beautiful young woman walked toward their table. "Nettie and Hank Carmichael, meet Annabelle Lemann. Her father owns the Lemann Boutique chain."

The niceties were exchanged, and Ralph helped Annabelle into her chair, then sat. Nettie waved for the waiter and ordered drinks all round.

"I was just saying how lovely it looks in here with all the decorations," Nettie said for Annabelle's benefit.

"It really does. They seemed to have gone all out," the newcomer said. "The lobby is nicely decorated as well. I'm surprised they haven't decorated the hallways too," she said with a smile.

Their drinks arrived, interrupting the conversation, and they were all handed menus. The food at the Sapphire Hotel was above reproach, and the best quality Nettie had ever eaten. For the price they charged, she expected nothing less. Father had often stayed here on business trips, and always talked up their service and the food. She could see why now.

Having someone special to share her time here made it even better.

After dinner, they sat around chatting, until Ralph could resist no longer. "I'm going up," he said, indicating the stage. "What about you?" His gaze was on Nettie, and she was torn. She knew Hank wouldn't like it, and besides, she wasn't in costume.

"I'm going to pass," she said reluctantly.

"Your loss," Ralph said, then walked to the stage amid applause. He flexed his fingers, then sat down and began to play.

"He really is good," Annabelle said.

Nettie felt like rolling her eyes. "He certainly is. Ralph had the best tuition money could buy."

Annabelle stared at her. "Of course. It was your father who paid for his lessons, wasn't it?"

"It was," Nettie said. "But it was Ralph who did all the hard work. He practiced for hours every day. My father was so proud of him." She swallowed back the emotion that threatened to overtake her and concentrated on Ralph's playing instead.

As if he knew what she was thinking, or at least how she felt, Hank squeezed her hand. It sent shivers down her spine. She vowed to enjoy Ralph's music – it was incredibly mesmerizing.

When he finished playing, Ralph stood and took a bow, then glanced across at Nettie. His hand extended as though asking her to join him. She felt Hank stiffen as he continued to hold her hand.

Hank was annoyed, but he had no need.

She stood, and the dining-room erupted in applause. Nettie took a sip of water, and she joined her friend on the stage. "One song, and one only," she whispered, then named the song she would sing. She glanced across at her husband. He was quietly fuming, and she send him an air kiss. His mood suddenly changed.

"This song is for my wonderful husband, Hank Carmichael," she said, then waited for Ralph to begin playing. When she opened her mouth and sang the first few words, the crowd erupted again. The room was electric – this was what kept her and Ralph coming back to perform time after time. It was disheartening when it didn't happen. They would be more selective about where they performed from now on.

If they had a choice, she was certain Ralph would agree. The Sapphire Hotel was the perfect location for them to perform long-term.

"Thank you, everyone. You are a wonderful audience," Nettie said as the pair bowed for their audience. They held hands, then hugged. The crowd erupted again. Ralph walked Nettie back to her seat, where Hank stood and hugged her as well.

"You were wonderful," he whispered. "You were both wonderful," he said louder for everyone at their table to hear.

Ralph pierced him with his eyes. "Nettie is always wonderful. I've never heard anyone better."

"I agree," Hank said.

Nettie's eyes went from one man to the other. Was this some kind of slinging match? It wasn't like she was available. She and Hank were legally married, and they had consummated their marriage many times over. Ralph was totally aware of that fact.

Nettie hoped Annabelle turned out to be the one for Ralph. She'd like nothing more than to see her friend as happy as she was.

Chapter Ten

The two couples walked back to their rooms together. They dropped Annabelle off at her room along the way. Hank and Nettie walked ahead, giving the pair time alone. Then Ralph caught up.

"I'm sorry I behaved like a spoiled brat," Ralph said, surprising Hank. "I guess I was worried for Nettie."

Hank turned to face him. "In what way? I would never harm her. I thought you knew that."

Ralph seemed to think before answering. "I didn't think you would. I wasn't convinced neither of you loved the other." He stared at Hank, who found it rather unsettling. "I was concerned you were a gold-digger."

Hank chuckled then. "You and Nettie both. I assure you, I'm not interested in her money. Claude Dupont paid me far more than I'll ever need, despite my protests. His retainer alone was more money than I'd seen in the entire previous year."

Nettie and Ralph glanced at each other.

"Terrible, isn't it? I told him I didn't need so much money, but he insisted. Every month, he paid more into my bank account. The worst of it is, he died before I located Nettie, so was unaware she'd been found safe and well."

He glanced across at his wife. Tears danced on her lashes. It was a difficult time for her, and he really should avoid talking about her father. She seemed to cope until they discussed him again. "I'm sorry, sweetheart," he whispered, then pulled her close. Hank kissed her forehead, trying to comfort her.

Ralph was watching them closely. *Was he still unconvinced they weren't in love?* No matter, they didn't need his approval.

Suddenly, they heard shouting. Hank hurried Nettie into their room. "Can you stay here and watch out for Nettie?" he asked Ralph hurriedly. "I need to check that out."

Ralph locked the door behind him, then Hank ran back down the corridor toward the shouting. He was relieved to find it was two teenage boys, likely brothers, having a disagreement. He had been promised the wrong type of people couldn't get into the Sapphire Hotel, but it suddenly hit him – what if they were the wrong sort of people, pretending to be the right type?

Hank shook his head. With the little he'd learned about Buster Macklin, there was virtually no money available to throw about. The last thing he could do was to afford a room at the prestigious Sapphire

Hotel. Nettie's distant cousin didn't seem to be the resourceful type, especially when it came to money, so Hank decided he was worrying for nothing.

He shook his head, trying to clear his mind, then headed back to their room. Nettie was safe here, and the sooner he believed that, the better.

Unfortunately, Hank was certain her cousin wouldn't give up so easily. Not with so much at stake.

"Hank," Nettie said later that night. They both lay in bed, and he held her close. As close as he could possibly get. He leaned in and kissed her neck. "It's not too late, you know."

"Too late for what?" he asked as his lips connected with her skin.

She rolled over to face him and leaned in to kiss his lips. "To go to the music hall."

Hank sighed. *Not this again. Would she never give up?*

"There has been no sign of Buster, and it appears to be safe." She leaned forward and kissed him again. If Nettie thought she could win him over with her affections, she was wrong. "We still have plenty of time to get there." She stared into his face, and he couldn't help but gaze into her hazel colored eyes.

Or her lips. It took all his effort to resist those pouting lips. But he did.

Momentarily.

His arms went up around her, and Nettie was like putty in his arms. He kissed her deeply and pulled her closer.

"What do you think, Hank?" she asked dreamily.

"Anything you say, Nettie," he responded. Then froze. *What just happened? Had his wife become a manipulator?* He mentally slapped his forehead. "I didn't…"

"You are such a wonderful husband," she said, then kissed him again. Hank was far too involved in what he was doing to argue. His wife was intoxicating, and right now, that's all he wanted to think about.

Several days had passed, and arrangements made for them to travel to the Royal Imperial Music Hall. Hank regretted the conversation, but had promised Nettie, and couldn't go back on his word. It was one performance, on one night only. Hank couldn't see what all the fuss was about, but according to Nettie, it was their livelihood at stake.

Not that she needed to worry about money. Never again in her life would money be an issue. Ralph, on the other hand, was the concern. Still, his wife was determined the pair would continue to perform together for many years to come.

It was not something he was happy about, especially if Buster Macklin was not found and locked away.

The knock at their hotel room door disrupted Hank's thoughts. "Good morning, Walter," Hank greeted the hotel manager.

"Good morning, Sir. The hansom cab is here, and the Pullman Carriage booked for three. I have made arrangements for both your rooms here at the Sapphire Hotel to be reserved until you return."

"Excellent," Hank said. That way they could leave the belongings they didn't require, as well as know their room was secured. "I don't want anyone entering our rooms while we're gone. No one," he reiterated, then handed Walter a one hundred-dollar bill. The other man's eyes opened in amazement.

"Thank you, Sir, but you don't have to do that." He pushed the money back into Hank's hand.

Hank was becoming irritated. "My wife and I want to thank you for all your help. Consider it a Christmas bonus," he said, shoving the money back again.

"Please accept our gift," Nettie said sweetly as she came up behind her husband. "We will be offended if you don't."

A brief smile crossed Walter's lips. "In that case, how can I refuse?" he said, and shook Hank's hand.

It was a small price to pay to ensure their belongings were not interfered with, and no one entered the rooms. "Can I assume all keys to our rooms will be with you, and only you?"

"Most definitely," Walter said. "I have arranged for a porter to load your luggage in the cab," he said. "Your cab is ready when you are." He smiled, then strode away. Hank was certain he saw a skip in the man's step.

With Nettie on his arm, Hank knocked on Ralph's door. "Time to go," he called, and waited momentarily for the other man to leave his room. They went to the lobby together.

"What are you going to do without Annabelle?" Nettie asked as they passed the other woman's hotel room.

"I'll miss her for sure, but we'll only be gone a few days." Ralph shrugged his shoulders then, as if admitting he wasn't certain if their relationship would last the distance.

"The making up is always good," Hank said, raising his eyebrows. Nettie punched him on the arm and glared at him.

Hank had never traveled in the Pullman Car before, and the extravagance of it was overwhelming. He thought he'd seen it all at the Sapphire Hotel, but this was every bit on par with the hotel.

The car was exclusive to certain patrons, and the steward ensured everyone was looked after appropriately. The moment they arrived on board the train, they were guided to the lounge, where they were seated in luxurious chairs, then offered tea and coffee. Their luggage was taken by porters who delivered it to their sleeping quarters.

If Hank thought they were coddled at the Sapphire Hotel, compared to this, he was wrong. Ralph appeared to be as enamored as Hank was. "Might I offer you cake, Sir?" Their steward, Thomas, asked.

"Not for me, thank you," Hank replied. It wasn't long since they'd had breakfast.

Thomas moved from Hank to Nettie, and then to Ralph. "I will announce luncheon," Thomas continued, "which will be served at noon sharp. If you require further refreshments, please let me know." Then he was gone.

"It's all a bit fancy," Ralph whispered.

"It would want to be," Hank returned. "It's pricey, but said to be worth it. Besides, Nettie should be safe in here."

His wife sighed. "I think my cousin has given up. There's been no sign of him in all this time."

Hank studied her. Nettie really was convinced it was safe for her now. He was the opposite. In his opinion, Buster was leading them on, letting them think he'd given up. Then, boom! He would pounce. That's what worried Hank the most. He was certain the man would come out of nowhere and pounce. He had the advantage of Hank not knowing what he looked like.

Was he short or tall, dark haired or blond? Was he skinny or fat, pock-faced or did he have unblemished skin? These were all questions he'd like answers to, but had none. Because of his upbringing, there were no family photographs. Had he been left with his mother, more than likely his life would have been documented with many photographs. Being taken away by his father to live with his grandparents, meant the boy did not enjoy the luxuries money could buy him. Hank was convinced it was the reason Buster was determined to kill Nettie and get her inheritance.

A shudder went through him. He couldn't bear the thought of her cousin getting close to Nettie. Losing her was not optional. He would have to be diligent – even here on the Pullman Car where it was meant to be safe and secure. Hank would like nothing more than to sit back and relax and enjoy their brief stay here, but it was not possible.

He promised Claude Dupont to look after his daughter. He'd gone above and beyond that promise already, but Hank was determined to keep Nettie from harm's way, even if it meant losing his own life. He loved her more than he ever thought possible.

Hank was startled by the clatter of… what? He wasn't sure, but was on his feet in seconds. He was furious with himself for drifting off to sleep. He had to keep alert for Nettie's sake.

"Did you have a nice nap?" Nettie asked, smiling up at him. "Lunch will be ready soon."

"My apologies, Sir," Thomas said. Hank had no idea where the man surfaced from. He seemed to come out of nowhere. "The help dropped some rather noisy trays. Lunch will be served shortly."

Hank automatically reached for his gun, but let his hand relax at the revelation. Nettie frowned at him. "We're safe in here," she said quietly.

"It's you I'm worried about," he said firmly. "I'm not convinced about how safe it is."

Thomas turned back and stood beside Hank. "Your wife is safe here, Sir. We have a train detective in this car. He is armed, and will shoot anyone who tries to harm Mrs. Carmichael, or anyone else in this carriage."

"You see," Nettie said. "What did I tell you?" Nettie seemed so carefree and unaware of the danger. Hank was not so naïve. He knew the ways of criminals, and those who lived a dark life. His wife did not.

A few minutes later, Thomas returned. "Luncheon is served. Please make your way into the dining car." He indicated where they should go, and Hank hooked his arm through Nettie's, ensuring she was close by at all times.

Chapter Eleven

It all seemed like a dream.

Nettie was certain she'd traveled on the Pullman Car before, but it was so long ago, her memory of it was vague. Mother was still alive then, so it had to be when she was very young.

She was glad all three of them got to experience it together. She'd hate to do it alone.

"This food is amazing," Ralph said. Hank grinned. They had become accustomed to the delicious food at the Sapphire Hotel, but who would have guessed meals served on a train could be so scrumptious?

"It certainly is," Hank said as soon as he'd swallowed down the mouthful of apple pie he was enjoying. "I would never tell her, but this is better than my mother made." He chuckled then.

"It would never do to tell her that," Nettie told him, then suddenly clamped her mouth shut. Was Hank's mother even alive? She had no idea. She'd been married to him for a few weeks now, but didn't know anything about him. Except, of course, her father trusted him with her life. That was enough of a recommendation for her.

Knowing Claude Dupont, he would have had Hank checked out thoroughly. He would have chosen him on two criteria: he was down on his luck, and he was trustworthy. That was all that mattered to her father. He was pedantic about those two things. If a person was untrustworthy, Father would not deal with them. It was the reason she had trusted Hank from the very start.

Until she began to have doubts. She'd let her imagination run away, and look where it got her. How on earth could she even think her wonderful husband could be a killer? The thought was laughable. She was lucky he didn't have her placed in a lunatic asylum. Women have been dumped in those places for far less.

That thought made her pause. But only for a moment. She had already established her husband was who he said he was. If he had intended to do something along those lines, he could have already done it and not played out this complicated scenario. He'd even proven everything he'd told her with the paperwork.

Paperwork that could have been created to prove himself.

Urgh! *Was she going crazy? Was all this cloak and dagger stuff getting to her?*

As though he could look into her mind, Hank reached across the table and covered her hand. "Everything alright?" he asked, concern on his face.

"I'm a little tired," she said, not willing to disclose her ridiculous thoughts. Not for a second time. Hank had more than convinced her he was truly to be trusted. Nettie mentally shook herself. Father would not have trusted Hank without good reason, and that's what she needed to do. No more second guessing him, or concerning herself. Hank was a good man. He was the last person you would expect to be a criminal.

And if he wasn't? What then? He had total control over her father's estate, and there wasn't a thing Nettie could do about it.

The handsom cab dropped them at the door of the Royal Imperial Hotel, in downtown San Francisco. The Royal Imperial Music Hall was right next door. From the moment they'd stepped outside the Sapphire Hotel, the music hall paid for everything. It made Nettie realize her worth as a performer. She was certain Ralph would feel the same. They were also being paid a very reasonable fee, but as she'd tried to explain to Hank, none of that mattered.

It was the prestige of performing there. It was a once-in-a-lifetime opportunity. You could not approach them, they approached you. It made her think it was probably time they secured a manager. Someone who would arrange their bookings from now on.

No longer were the pair amateurs. Performing here put them into the big league. When all of this was over, she would look into it. She would breach the subject with Ralph, but was almost certain he would agree.

Nettie pulled her thick coat up around herself and tightened her scarf. "It's really chilly here," she said. "It's easy to tell it's almost Christmas." Glancing about, the ground had a light covering of snow. Not enough to build a snowman – it was far from that. There was, however, enough snow for a person to slip and land on their backside, and do some decent damage. They'd got this far, and Nettie had no intention of letting that happen one day before their performance.

The driver removed their small amount of luggage, and the hotel porter took it from him. "This way, Sirs, Madam," he said, and they all followed him inside.

"Mr. and Mrs. Carmichael, and Mr. Hanover," Hank told the receptionist. Nettie brushed the light layer of snow from her coat, and was startled when someone came up behind her.

"My apologies, Madam," the Concierge said. "I didn't mean to startle you. Let me help you out of your wet coat." He took it from her without further ado. "I will have it dried and returned to you." He nodded his head, but lingered. "Shall I book your group into the dining-room for this evening's meal?"

She gazed at Hank. He would decide, that had become very clear over the past weeks. She pleaded with her eyes, and he pulled her close. Hank kissed her forehead, then answered the Concierge. "That would be wonderful," he said. "We're looking forward to it." He passed over a bill, and the other man smiled.

"Consider it done."

Nettie glanced about. The Royal Imperial Hotel was every bit as luxurious as the Sapphire Hotel, but didn't feel as homely. The fact they'd lived at the latter for some weeks probably helped with that. They wouldn't be at this hotel for more than a few days, so no chance of them settling in there as they'd done at the other hotel.

She stared at the ornamental staircase. It was covered with a luxurious red patterned carpet that matched the rest of the lobby. The front desk was crafted with mahogany and was highly polished. The chandeliers were beautifully designed and gave the place a prestigious feel.

Everything thing about this hotel was high class. Nettie expected their rooms would be equally as good.

"Ah, here is the porter with your luggage," the Concierge said. "He will accompany you to your room."

Nettie was certain with the size of the tip Hank had given the man, their every wish would be fulfilled.

"Thank you for your help," Hank said. "It is appreciated."

The Concierge nodded his head. "Enjoy your stay." He turned and walked away then, and the group followed the porter up the stairs to their rooms.

Hank stayed closed to Nettie. She appreciated it, but didn't feel at all threatened here. They didn't appear to have the high level of security the Sapphire Hotel had, but looks could be deceiving. This hotel had high-profile guests on a regular basis, just as the other establishment did. Many of the guests here would likely be of a higher class, since many would perform at the music hall. Until their booking, Nettie was unaware the music hall and hotel were owned by the same entity, despite the similar name.

She glanced across at her husband, and he appeared to be deep in thought. Knowing Hank, he was likely checking out all likely hiding places, and making a plan for tomorrow night. She knew it was a risk, but the risk was all hers. Buster Macklin was not interested in Ralph, so he was safe.

More than anything, Nettie wished her cousin had contacted her. Nettie would happily pay the man a generous allowance, and she knew her father would. Buster was Claude Dupont's great nephew. According to Hank, when Buster's father took the boy when he was only a toddler, the family lost touch. With no clue on where he was, he was not seen again.

It was a sad situation for all concerned, but most of all, his mother. As far as Hank could discover, she never saw her son again after that terrible day.

"Everything alright?" Hank's voice brought Nettie out of her thoughts. How could she ever think her husband was anything but above board? He always had her best interests at heart and looked out for her. If he was the gold-digger, she imagined he could be, Hank could easily have killed her off by now. With his background, he could make it look like an accident and no one would be any the wiser.

She smiled up at him. "Just thinking about Buster and what a terrible life he must have had to turn out the way he has."

"It is sad, but don't feel sorry for him. Buster made his choices, and look where that got him."

Nettie understood, but there were two sides to every story. "I can't help but think about how he might have turned out if he was part of the Dupont family. His life could have been so much different. Aunt Miranda was not as wealthy as my father, but she would have looked after her grandson, if she'd been given the chance."

"Your father would have helped, I'm certain." Hank seemed a little sad as he thought about Nettie's dear father.

"Enough of sad things. We need to do something fun." Nettie did not want to get down in the dumps. She wanted to celebrate this happy time in their lives. "What can we do in this magnificent hotel?"

"You could have a bath," Hank suggested, then moved closer. "I could join you," he added quietly, and she punched his arm.

"A bath is not a bad idea, but I prefer my baths alone."

Hank grinned. "I will arrange it then."

Chapter Twelve

Nettie opened her eyes and stretched her arms as she greeted the new day. A soak in a hot bath was exactly what she needed.

Today was the day of their performance at the Royal Imperial Music Hall. Her heart pounded. Ralph and Nettie had been working toward this for as long as she could remember. Teenagers when they met, they'd made a secret pact of this goal.

It had taken a decade, but they finally got there. Her father would be so proud. He wanted nothing more than for Nettie to be happy. He had a soft spot for Ralph as well. He was like the son Claude Dupont had never had. Providing piano lessons for him was the one thing that got Ralph on track. He had to commit himself to practicing every day, and that had to be done at the Dupont home.

Without Claude Dupont, who knew where Ralph would be right now? Likely in a similar position to Buster Macklin. The thought of it broke Nettie's heart.

"Good morning," Nettie said quietly, leaning over her husband as he slept. He was such a handsome man and trustworthy. Nettie did not know why she had pockets of time where she doubted him. Hank had done nothing to earn her mistrust, and yet… now and then she suspected him of wrongdoing.

Hank's eyes remained closed, but his arms suddenly wrapped around her, pulling Nettie close against him. His lips suddenly covered hers, and he opened his eyes slowly. "Good morning, my love," he said. His words sounded genuine, and Nettie once again had no reason to disbelieve he meant everything he said.

He rolled over, taking Nettie with him, until she was underneath him. A smile played on his lips, and Nettie was lost in the moment.

She would have preferred breakfast in the dining-room, but Hank insisted they have it in their room – only the two of them. They needed time alone, he said, and she knew Hank was right. Ralph was their third wheel, and it got rather tiresome at times. Nettie wished they'd brought Annabelle along with them, but likely she would have refused. The young woman had a reputation to protect, just as Nettie had. It was the very reason she'd married Hank.

She smiled. Marrying Hank was the best thing she could have done. It might have been a marriage of convenience in the beginning, but things had changed quickly. Apart from being very good to look at, Hank was charismatic. He was the sort of person you warmed to quickly. She could imagine her father when he met Hank. Claude Dupont loved people. Once he decided he liked someone, he spent as much time as possible with them.

He would shower them with gifts. Often those gifts would be in the form of money. Hank had mentioned her father kept paying money into his bank account. It wasn't like Father couldn't afford it – he was worth millions. But sometimes people took advantage of his kindness. She couldn't imagine Hank doing that.

"Later, we'll go to the music hall and check it out. I need to ensure security is tight."

Nettie stared at him. Surely the danger was passed? "You don't honestly think Buster is going to come after me there?"

Hank covered her hand. "I don't know anything, and that's the problem. He hasn't shown himself since he…" He paused, and Nettie instinctively knew Hank was going to say 'since he murdered your father.'

Emotion threatened to bubble up and overtake her once again, but Nettie fought the urge. It never got easier.

Tonight's performance was for Father. She prayed he would be looking down and approving of the performance the pair would do tonight. They would play to a packed house – she'd been informed tickets were already sold out. It was yet another reason they had to turn up. There was no way Nettie was going to turn down the opportunity to play to a packed house.

"I need to familiarize myself with the stage, and Ralph needs to practice on the piano. It's no good either of us just turning up tonight." She watched Hank for his reaction. He hadn't been keen on them going, let alone spending more time there than he thought was necessary.

But this was necessary. It was a genuine part of what they needed to do. "I can understand that. We will lock the place up, and no one will enter who doesn't belong there."

That made perfect sense. It made Nettie feel better, too. She would dearly love to take a stroll in downtown San Francisco today, but already knew Hank would balk at such a blatant disregard for her safety. She loved he felt that way.

"I've heard San Francisco has wonderful shops. Women's boutiques especially." She didn't have a vast wardrobe, far from it. It wasn't that her clothes were threadbare, but they weren't in the best condition. She had to look the part, especially now she had taken over her father's business.

"No downtown shopping. It's far too dangerous."

Nettie pouted, and Hank frowned. He leaned forward and kissed her gently. "I'll arrange for someone to come in today and outfit you."

That would have to do. After all, what choice did she have?

~*~

It didn't take long, and was soon was all hustle and bustle. A word with the Concierge, and soon a rack of beautiful gowns arrived for Nettie to choose from. She eventually chose a selection of gowns for her daily use, as well as one gown that would work with her performance.

The dressmaker needed to make some minor changes, but promised to return with at least two of the gowns this afternoon. She needed to make adjustments to her work gown, and they were more time-consuming.

The woman definitely knew what she was doing, which pacified Nettie. She was concerned that making last-minute arrangements would produce inferior results. Father always told her if something was worth getting, then she had to ensure it was the best quality available.

Nettie felt bad ordering so many gowns, but she moved around far too much to want to worry about laundering often. Staying in hotels like this one meant it wasn't so much an issue, but that wouldn't always be the case, she was certain.

Out of the way hotels didn't offer laundering to their hotel guests, which made it rather awkward. After tonight, she hoped they would be in great demand, which would mean moving about even more often than they had before.

If Buster Macklin was arrested, that was.

Nettie sighed. She didn't want to think about the weeks and months ahead if her cousin was not caught and jailed. Living like a fugitive did not make her happy. She was not the one in the wrong. Buster was. But she was paying the price for his crimes. It wasn't fair, but nothing Nettie could do about it.

"I will return at three o'clock, if that works for you," the dressmaker, Esther Padlow, said.

They had a small window where they could attend the music hall for Hank to check things out, such as security, and for Nettie to do a quick practice run on the stage. Ralph would also ensure the piano was to his liking. Apart from that, they would be available. Nettie glanced at Hank, who nodded. "That sounds perfect," she said.

"Wonderful. I will also return tomorrow morning with the rest of your order. Does nine o'clock suit you?"

Esther left them alone after they agreed on a time, and Nettie contemplated the situation. "I can't believe this is finally happening." She shook her head. "It feels like a dream. Is this real?" she asked Hank. She could barely believe they were married, let alone she would perform at the Royal Imperial Music Hall – a place she'd dreamed of performing at for many, many years.

"It's a dream come true, is what it is," he said, grinning broadly. Then answered the knock at the door.

"Morning tea for two," the room service waiter said. They hadn't ordered room service, and Hank balked. He glanced at the curtain that surrounded the trolley.

His hand automatically moved to his gun, and Nettie gasped. *Had Buster finally caught up with them? But how did he get into the hotel?*

She looked him over. The man standing in front of Hank appeared disheveled. There was no way anyone working for the Royal Imperial Hotel would be permitted to attend to hotel guests looking like this.

She stared at his face. Nettie could see features of Aunt Miranda in this man. "It's him," she shouted.

Hank's gun was out of its holster before the other man could reach for his gun. "Don't even think about it," Hank said firmly. "Nettie, fetch Ralph, quickly."

She ran past the two men and collected her friend as directed. Ralph used a shoe lace to tie the other man up, then ran downstairs to bring the Concierge.

"Where did you get this uniform?" the Concierge demanded when he arrived, but Buster Macklin refused to answer. Instead, his eyes pierced Nettie. "It's all *her* fault," he shouted, and Nettie cringed. *How could it be her fault?*

Hank pushed Nettie back into the room, then checked the man's badge. "Ted McLean. Do you know him?" he asked the Concierge.

"I certainly do, and this is not Ted," he said. "What have you done to Ted?" The Concierge was upset now, worried about one of his staff.

Hank shoved the man and forced him downstairs. The Concierge wanted him out of sight of the other guests, but Nettie was certain Hank wanted a place to grill the man.

Ralph went downstairs with Nettie. She was distraught over the missing man. She couldn't live with herself if Buster had killed him. Even if he was injured, she would not be happy. *Why did he have to draw innocent people into his circle of evil?*

Ralph sat Nettie down in the lobby, where someone brought her tea. Her nerves were shot. *How could they perform tonight?* So much for having a quiet day, but this was a better outcome than to have Buster shoot at her on stage. She would have hated if he'd tried to shoot her and hit Ralph instead. Nettie could never live with herself.

It seemed like forever before the police arrived, and just as long before they found the missing man. The real Ted McLean was found tied and gagged in the basement, locked in a closet. Without a thorough search, he could have been there for days.

"I'm so sorry," Nettie told Ted McLean over and over. The man held no malice toward her, for which Nettie was very grateful. Despite his protests, she insisted the doctor was called. Nettie was grateful the man had no injuries apart from rope burns to his wrists, but he was, of course, quite shaken.

Buster Macklin was taken into custody by the police and arrested. "You were never going to get away with it," Hank told the man.

Nettie couldn't help but study her cousin. "All you had to do was ask for help," Nettie said, forcing herself not to feel anger toward this man. "Father would have helped you, and so would I."

"Your father," he shouted, "wanted proof I was Buster Macklin. What sort of way is that to treat your great nephew?" Fury clouded his face.

"It's exactly what I would have done," Hank told him calmly.

"That still didn't give you the right to kill him," Nettie said, tears dancing on her eyelashes. "We would have welcomed you into the family. If you want to blame anyone, blame your own father for taking you away from your mother and the Dupont family." It was Buster's turn to study Nettie then. "We could have been friends. Right now, I never want to see you again." She took a fortifying breath before speaking again. "I hope you rot in hell."

The police marched Buster out of the hotel and into the waiting police wagon.

She turned to Hank then, who cradled her against his chest. Her ordeal was over, at least until the trial. "I'm sorry, Hank," she whispered, to ensure no one else could hear. "I should never have suspected you. You are my rock, my everything. I love you far more than I ever thought it possible to love another person."

"I know," he whispered against her ear. "I love you too."

Chapter Thirteen

The rehearsal seemed to go well so far, and despite knowing Buster was behind bars, Hank searched every nook and cranny before allowing Nettie to rehearse. Despite his refusal to the confirm either way, who knew if Buster had a back-up? Hank wasn't going to take the risk with his wife's life.

The Concierge ensured their every request was met. He somehow seemed to blame himself. He told Hank he should have spotted the imposter wandering around the hotel. The fact the Concierge was kept busy attending to each guest's individual needs did not seem to appease him.

Hank stood to the side of the stage, out of view of the audience. This was the very spot he would place himself tonight. He couldn't wait. He'd now seen this pair perform, but to see and hear the accolades they deserved would be spectacular.

Nettie had been through quite a lot today, and he worried about her state of mind. It was the last thing she needed on her big day.

"Ralph wants to spend some time familiarizing himself with the piano and get the chair to the correct height for tonight," Nettie said. "Shall you and I go down there?" she asked, indicating the area the audience sat.

They climbed down the few steps together. "How are you feeling?" Hank asked. She was still quite pale. Not that he blamed her. He would insist she rest once they finished here. Nettie had waited for this day for such a long time. He only wished Claude Dupont could be there to see her perform.

At least now his killer was found, and Nettie was safe. Hank knew that would be the most important thing to her father. His daughter's safety always came first.

As her husband, Hank would ensure her father's last wish was granted.

Nettie reluctantly agreed to rest. She slept for a few hours before her new costume for tonight was due to arrive. Several of the other gowns she had also chosen should be with them.

Her face lit up the moment Hank opened the door and she saw Esther standing there. The Concierge was also there, along with one of the porters, who had guided the clothing rack to their room.

"Come in, come in," Nettie said. She was still half asleep, but her enthusiasm came through clearly. Esther removed her new costume from the rack and held it up for Nettie to examine. "It's beautiful,"

Nettie exclaimed. "It's been a long time since I began using my old costume." She held the new gown up against her and studied herself in the mirror. "I need to try it on," she decided. "You men all need to leave."

They all left except Hank. She pouted and stared at him. "What? I have to leave too? But I'm your husband," he protested, and both the women laughed. Nettie chased him out of the room.

Esther helped Nettie out of the gown she was wearing. "I heard what happened this morning," she said gently. "Are you alright? It must have been a terrifying experience." The older woman patted her hand. "I'm sorry," she suddenly said. "It is none of my business.

Nettie was touched Esther cared enough to ask. "I am rather shaken, but otherwise, I'm fine. I am more concerned about the worker who was accosted. Thank goodness he was not harmed."

Esther nodded as she studied the gown. "Can you take a few steps, please? Like you would on the stage. I need to ensure you can move about as you need to."

Nettie slid across the room. She bent forward and she stretched her arms. She stepped out across the room, as she would normally do on stage. The gown was perfect. She was pleased it fitted perfectly. "You have done a wonderful job," she told Esther.

"You came highly recommended, and I can see why." She leaned in and hugged the other woman. "I want to personally thank you for ensuring I had this costume back on time for tonight's performance. Not that the audience could see from where they sit, but the old one was becoming quite scruffy. You must have noticed it when I showed you the costume this morning."

She watched as Esther decided to be truthful or not. "It's alright, Esther. I know it's in terrible condition. I should have replaced it far sooner. What you have created is even better than the original." She handed the woman an envelope.

Esther stared at it warily. "I don't usually take cash," she said. "I'll send an account."

"Of course I still expect you to send an account, but this is not money. It's something money cannot buy. There are two tickets to tonight's performance in that envelope. It's a sold-out performance, but I thought you might like to attend, along with a friend or your husband, if you have one."

Esther squealed and put her hands to her mouth. "Oh, Mrs. Carmichael, thank you so much," she said between tears. "It would be an honor." She clutched the envelope to her chest, and Nettie felt warm all over.

Hank stood to the side of the stage as they'd discussed with the management. Nettie and Ralph stood next to him. While Nettie finished preparing for the performance, applying make up and fixing her hair, Hank stood guard. He would not let his guard down until the night was over.

Buster Macklin was locked up in jail, but Hank still wasn't taking any risks.

He'd checked the dressing rooms, the store room, and searched all the back-stage areas. Along with some of the hotel staff, he examined the entire auditorium where the audience would sit. He wasn't taking any chances. Nettie said it was overkill, but he'd rather that than have his wife slain.

They still had no confirmation Buster was working alone. He seemed the type who would refuse to admit guilt, even on his deathbed. That meant Hank needed to be extra vigilant.

Hank watched as the audience filed into the auditorium. His heart pounded. It wouldn't be long before everyone was seated, and the performance began. He could only imagine how Nettie and Ralph were feeling right now.

"Ten minutes," the stage manager told them, and Hank nodded.

"Nervous?" Hank asked his wife.

"Terrified," she said, but outwardly she seemed calm. "What about you, Ralph?"

He held out a hand, and they watched it shake. "I'll be fine," he said. "I'm always like this before a performance." Hank had not realized that was the case. Ralph never appeared nervous and was obviously good at covering it up. "Don't worry about me, Hank," Ralph said as he hugged Nettie. "This is what we've worked for all these years. We'll kill it," he whispered.

Hank was certain they would. The pair were professionals and knew exactly what they were doing.

"And now, ladies and gentlemen," the Master of Ceremonies announced. "Let me introduce the renowned Ivory and Melodies – Miss Nettie Dupont, and Mr. Ralph Hanover."

The room erupted in applause, and the entire auditorium was electric. Hank was overcome with emotion. Ralph walked onto the stage, and Nettie followed, but turned back briefly to kiss her husband. "I love you," she said, then hurried onto the stage.

Hank watched in awe as the audience stood and applauded. Not a key had been played, not a word had been sung. Until this moment, he had no idea how popular these two really were. Sure, he'd seen them perform, but only in the dining-room of the Sapphire Hotel.

This is where they belonged – on a stage built for the purpose. His heart pounded. Hank knew they were both nervous. Nettie had told him repeatedly this was their big break, but he did not know how important it really was. Now it was all happening in front of him, and he finally recognized the significance of it to them both.

He watched as they stood facing the audience. They held hands and bowed. The pair stood there until the crowd died down, then Ralph took his place at the piano, flexing his fingers in preparation.

The room was so quiet you could hear a pin drop. The tension was building. Nettie took her place on the stage. Once again, she had seamlessly taken the feathered fan from the piano and stood with her back to the audience, waiting for her queue.

Ever so slowly, she turned as she sang. The fan sliding down her face and resting slightly above her bosom.

The room erupted, applause broke out, but she ignored it all. A shy smile cut across her face, but there was little other sign of her joy. Hank knew her all too well and could see she was elated. Ralph had his back to Hank, but he was certain Ralph, too, would be filled with happiness.

Hank glanced out at the crowd from his little hideaway behind the curtains. "They're good," the stage manager told him. "I can't believe we haven't had them here before this."

"They are good," Hank said. "The best." He turned to the stage manager then. "That's my wife out there." He couldn't believe how much pride he felt. And relief at knowing she was safe.

She would always be safe with Hank. He would make sure of it.

The Master of Ceremonies returned to the stage at the end of the performance. "Ladies and Gentlemen, wasn't that amazing?" He turned to Nettie and handed her a bouquet of flowers. They were magnificent, and Nettie's face lit up.

The pair received a standing ovation, and Hank was in awe. They were amazing and so much more. The applause, the standing ovation, the whistling and shouting for more went on for about five minutes.

Finally, once the crowd died down, Nettie agreed to sing one more song. As Ralph began to play, Hank realized it was one he had not heard before.

Nettie outstretched her arm to him and indicated for Hank to come onto the stage with her. "Ladies and gentlemen, my husband, Hank Carmichael," she said, then sang a love song. She faced him as she sang, and it was as though he was the only person in the room instead of the hundreds that filled the auditorium.

At first, Hank's heart fluttered, but as she sang the words, so intimate, and seemingly only for his ears, his heart pounded. Did she mean those words? And did she really mean them for him and him alone? Hank loved her with all his being, and if her words were anything to go by, Nettie felt the same.

When the words ended, she pulled Hank close and hugged him. Then she kissed him, and the crowd was in an uproar. They applauded far harder than they had before, and there was another standing ovation.

"Miss Nettie Dupont," the Master of Ceremonies said, indicating Nettie. "Mr. Ralph Hanover," he said as Ralph stood. "Thank you both for a magnificent evening. It is one I will never forget," he said, then led them off the stage.

The applause continued, and the two went back onto the stage momentarily and bowed, then returned to the backstage again. Hank could not believe the response they had received. He could totally understand it, but if he hadn't witnessed it for himself, he would not have believed it.

How very proud her father would have been. He could only hope Claude Dupont was watching over his daughter tonight.

Nettie was happy to be back at the Sapphire Hotel. It felt like home. The Royal Imperial Hotel was equally as good with service and food, as so much more, but didn't have that same homely feeling. It probably didn't help that Buster Macklin had attempted to kill her there.

Two weeks had passed since their monumental performance at the music hall, but she was still trying to come down from the buzz. For several days, Hank had seemed rather overwhelmed by the entire experience, and had told her on several occasions her last song had astonished him. That one was special to her. It was a statement. It was meant to tell him how much in love she was with Hank, and she was thankful to have him in her life.

Nettie was pretty sure she had achieved that. Hank seemed different after that night. Previously she had admitted to not trusting him, to worrying about the fact *he* may have been the killer. Looking back, none of that made sense. He'd proven who he was, shown her all the paperwork, but still she was suspicious. Nettie knew now it was a product of circumstance. If she hadn't been so worried about someone trying to kill her, or so upset about her father's death…

She sat downstairs in the lobby with Hank, waiting to be called. Nettie wore one of her new gowns, her favorite of those made by Esther Padlow, back in San Francisco. The woman was amazing with a needle and thread. Nettie still couldn't believe the speed at which Esther had adjusted those beautiful gowns for her. If only she lived closer.

"They're ready," Walter Gawne, manager of the Sapphire Hotel, told them. The man grinned broadly. It wasn't something they saw often. "In here," he said, indicating the same room where Hank and Nettie had been married.

The preacher stood at the end of the room, his well-worn bible in his hands. Ralph stood to the right, and Annabelle to the left. She was resplendent in her wedding gown. Her parents followed them into the room. Nettie turned to comfort Annabelle's mother as she cried. Happy tears, Nettie was certain. After all, who wouldn't be happy for their daughter to marry a renowned pianist such as Ralph Hanover?

The preacher cleared his throat. "We are gathered here today," he said, and continued through the wedding ceremony. Nettie couldn't be more pleased to see Ralph so happy. He'd seemed like a lost soul since she and Hank had married, but since meeting Annabelle, he had come back to life.

Now she had found her soulmate, and Ralph had too. It was far more than she could have wished for. They were both happy, and had found their soulmates, who made their lives happier.

What more could they wish for?

Nettie was excited for Christmas Day.

It would be her first with Hank as her husband, and Ralph's first with Annabelle as his wife. They had decided to stay on at the Sapphire Hotel for Christmas Day, as it promised to be special.

Besides, they hadn't decided where they would live. Nettie wasn't sure she could move into her father's home, but was certain he'd want her to. It was at the back of her mind, but today, she just wanted to enjoy her time with friends.

The group of four sat around their favorite table in the dining-room, talking and laughing together. Annabelle had fitted into their circle well, and she and Annabelle were becoming good friends. Her parents joined them as well, and it was wonderful. Such a happy, friendly group of people.

Nettie glanced about. She'd watched as the hotel staff added more decorations around the building specifically for the celebrations, and they were beautiful. A beautifully decorated tree sat in the corner of the dining-room, and a far bigger one in the lobby. The place was so beautiful, Nettie never wanted to leave.

Despite all of the hard work that had been put in, one thing was missing.

Music.

Ralph glanced across at Nettie. "Shall we?" he asked, eyebrows raised.

"Why not?" Nettie said as she stood, then leaned in and kissed her husband, hoping that would appease him.

Hank glanced up at her. "You two can't help yourselves," he said as he chuckled.

Nettie glanced out the window. It was a perfect Christmas Day with snow, good food, but most importantly, good friends and people she loved.

Her only wish was her father could be here.

Ralph sat down at the piano. The dining-room staff had become so accustomed to the pair performing on a whim, they didn't even flinch when they began. Nettie noticed the manager arrive and sit down at their table. He seemed pretty happy.

Ralph played a few keys, and then Nettie sang. loud and clear. "O Holy Night," her words were loud and clear.

When the song was over, she turned to Ralph and hugged him. O Little Town of Bethlehem was next, and lastly, Angels We Have Heard On High.

The diners applauded and gave them a standing ovation. "Thank you everyone," Nettie said. "Ralph and I, along with our families, want to wish you all a love-filled Christmas." Then the pair returned to their table.

"Thank you. You didn't have to do that, today of all days," Walter Gawne told them, his smile almost splitting his face.

Nettie laughed. "We both wanted to. It's our gift to everyone here for making our lives better."

"That was truly beautiful," he said, still smiling.

Hank was beaming. "It certainly was. You two just get better and better." He leaned in then, and kissed Nettie on the lips. "Merry Christmas, my darling," he said.

"Merry Christmas, everyone," Nettie said. Apart from her father not being with them, it was a truly wonderful day.

Epilogue

Two years later…

Nettie stared out the window at the falling snow and sighed. She loved Christmas. What she didn't love was dress fittings. They never were her favorite thing to do.

This year would be special – their son, Claude, was experiencing his first Christmas. Nettie was beyond excited and was certain the toddler would be too, when Christmas Day came around.

"Just one more minute," Esther said with a pin in her mouth. "This gown really needs replacing," she said as she stared up at Nettie. "Perhaps we should make several versions of your costume. Each with extra room in a certain area?"

Nettie laughed, but knew deep down Esther wasn't joking. Her four-month baby bump made it almost impossible for Nettie to fit into her current costume. This was the second time Esther, who was now her personal dressmaker, had let this costume out.

When she was pregnant with Claude, Esther had designed a wrap that went around for her waist. It was made of the same material as the costume, and her audience didn't even realize she was pregnant.

"I am serious, Miss Nettie," Esther said. "It might not be too bad now, but in another couple of months, I won't be able to let it out enough."

"I know, believe me, I know." And she did. They should have done it last time around, but Nettie would have none of it. How many more babies would she have? No matter, it was incredibly difficult to perform with her stomach squashed under a tight costume. She'd had to stop performing last time when it got too uncomfortable. She wouldn't do it again, because it was unfair to Ralph. Not to mention her poor baby being all squashed up in her belly.

It wasn't that either of them needed the money; it was simply that they enjoyed performing. Nettie had been right all along about the Royal Imperial Music Hall. She was glad she'd insisted they attend. She was especially pleased Hank had agreed in the end. Otherwise, she would have had to adopt far more sneaky tactics to get there.

"Go ahead, Esther," Hank said. "As her manager, I am giving you permission." He chuckled then. Hank knew Nettie would agree after a while. Despite it being a repeat performance, she still hadn't got used to the fact her flat tummy was bulging again. Not that either of them would have it any other way.

Baby Claude scooted across the room, heading for the Christmas tree. Hank quickly scooped him up. "Mama," little Claude called, his arms outstretched. "I want my mama." His little eyes stared at her expectantly, but Hank held tight.

"Cuddle your baby," Esther said. "I can wait. Babies need their mamas." She smiled then, despite the adjustment required for tonight's performance.

With all the pins removed, Hank passed their son over. Nettie held him tight, and it wasn't long until Claude was sound asleep on her shoulder. Warmth filled her, and Nettie smiled at Hank. She reached out and held his hand.

As if she knew they needed some alone time, Esther left the room, leaving them alone.

Hank gently took their son and laid him in his crib in the next room. When he returned, he wrapped his wife in his arms. "I can't believe how much I love you," he whispered into her ear. "If fate hadn't stepped in, we wouldn't have even met." He pulled back then and stared into her eyes.

Hank was right. Fate, and her father, put the two together. How she could ever think Hank was involved in her father's death, Nettie would never know. What she knew was her life really began the day she met him.

Neither of them wanted or needed her father's money. She'd installed a trustworthy manager to run Claude Dupont's business, and to continue his charity work. Ensuring young people had a good start in life had been important to her father, and if Ralph was any indication of the likely outcome, she never wanted it to end.

Nettie leaned her head on her husband's shoulder. "Our visitors will be here shortly," she whispered. "We better get Esther back in to finish up."

Moments later, Ralph and Annabelle arrived. Nettie went to Anabelle to coo over their six-month-old daughter. She patted her own stomach – she couldn't wait for their new baby to arrive. She loved performing, and so did Ralph, but more than anything, they all adored their children and each other.

Nettie silently prayed her thanks to her father for sending her guardian angel – Hank Carmichael, the love of her life.

From the Author

Thank you so much for reading my book – I hope you enjoyed it.

I would greatly appreciate you leaving a review where you purchased, even if it is only a one-liner. It helps to have my books more visible.

About the Author

Multi-published, award-winning and bestselling author Cheryl Wright, former secretary, debt collector, account manager, writing coach, and shopping tour hostess, loves reading.

She writes both historical and contemporary western romance, as well as romantic suspense.

She lives in Melbourne, Australia, and is married with two adult children and has six grandchildren. When she's not writing, she can be found in her craft room making greeting cards.

Links

Website: *http://www.cheryl-wright.com/*

Facebook Reader Group:
https://www.facebook.com/groups/cherylwrightauthor/

Join My Newsletter:

https://cheryl-wright.com/newsletter/
(and receive a free book)